THE GIRL FROM THE WELL

RIN CHUPECO

sourcebooks
fire

Published by Sourcebooks Fire, an imprint of Sourcebooks, Inc.
P.O. Box 4410, Naperville, Illinois 60567-4410
(630) 961-3900
Fax: (630) 961-2168
www.sourcebooks.com

Library of Congress Cataloging-in-Publication data is on file with the publisher.

Printed and bound in the United States of America.
WOZ 10 9 8 7 6 5 4 3 2 1

For Les—
who taught me that monsters need love, too.

CHAPTER ONE

FIREFLIES

I am where dead children go.

With other kinds of dead, it is different. Often their souls drift quietly away, like a leaf caught in the throes of a hidden whirlpool, slipping down without sound, away from sight. They roll and ebb gently with the tides until they sink beneath the waves and I no longer see where they go—like sputtering candlelight, like little embers that burn briefly and brightly for several drawn moments before their light goes out.

But they are not my territory. They are not my hunt.

And then there are the murdered dead. And they are peculiar, stranger things.

You may think me biased, being murdered myself. But my state of being has nothing to do with curiosity toward my own species, if we can be called such. We do not go gentle, as your poet encourages, into that good night.

We are the fates that people fear to become. We are what happens to good persons and to bad persons and to everyone in between.

Murdered deads live in storms without season, in time without flux. We do not go because people do not let us go.

The man refuses to let her go, though he does not know this yet. He is inside an apartment that smells of dirty cigarettes and stale beer. He sits on a couch and watches television, where a man tells jokes. But this man who wears a stained white shirt, with his pudgy arms and foul vapors, this man does not laugh. He has too much hair on his head and on his face and on his chest, and he is drinking from a bottle and not listening to anything but the alcohol in his thoughts. His mind tastes like sour wine, a dram of sake left out in the dark for too long.

There are other things inside this apartment that he owns. There are filthy jackets of shiny fabric (three). Empty bottles (twenty-one) dribble dregs of brown liquid onto the floor. Thin tobacco stalks (five) are grounded on a tiny tray, smoke curling over their stunted remains.

There are other things inside the apartment that he does not own. Small, pale pink scratches of cloth snagged against nails in the floorboards (three). A golden strand of hair, smothered within the confines of wood (one).

Something

    gurgles,

from somewhere nearby. It is a loud and sudden noise, and it penetrates through the haze of his inebriation, startling him.

The Stained Shirt Man turns his head to a nearby wall and shouts, "You better fix that fuckin' toilet tomorrow, Shamrock!"

mistaking one problem for another. If he is expecting a reply, he does not receive it, but he does not seem to care.

He does not look my way because he does not see me. Not yet.

But she does.

I can tell she has not been dead long. Her long, yellow hair hangs limply around her waist, her skin gray and brittle and bloated. The man drowned her quickly, so quickly that she does not realize it. This is why her mouth opens and closes, why she gulps at intervals like a starving fish, why she is puzzled at the way she does not breathe.

Her blue eyes look into mine from where I lie hidden, shrouded in shadow. An understanding passes between us for I, too, remember that terrible weight of water. Her prison had been of ceramic, mine wrought from cobbled stones. In the end, it made little difference to either of us.

The Stained Shirt Man does not see her, either. He does not notice the thin, bony arms clasped about his neck, or the manner in which her little rag dress is hiked up above her hips, her legs balanced against the small of his back. He does not notice the beginnings of decay that are ravaging a face that should have been delicate and pretty.

Many people are like him; they do not feel burdened by the weight of those they kill. A rope braid around her thin wrist is attached to another folded over the man's arm. I wear a similar loop around my wrist, though unlike her, I endure this affliction with no one else. The rope trails several feet behind me, the edges shorn.

The man talking from inside the television disappears, and the thrum of static buzzes at the Stained Shirt Man's consciousness, nagging at him like an angry bee. Cursing again, he tosses his empty bottle away and strides to the box, fiddling with the dials. After a minute, he pounds a fist down on top of it once, twice, three times. The television continues to hum, unimpressed.

He is still angry when the lights in the room wink out one by one, leaving him nothing for company but the still-fizzling box.

"Son of a bitch!" he says, kicking it for good measure. As punishment, the noises stop and the television flickers back on, but the man telling jokes is nowhere to be seen. Instead, for a few seconds, something else flashes across the screen.

It is a wide, staring

    eye

and it is looking back at him.

It disappears, though the buzzing continues. The man gapes. He is afraid at first—that delicious fear steals across his face—but when the image does not repeat itself soon, he begins to think and then to argue and then to dismiss, the way people do when they are seeking explanations for things that cannot be explained.

"Must have imagined it," he mutters to himself, rubbing at his temple and belching. The girl on his back says nothing.

The Stained Shirt Man moves to the bathroom and frowns when he turns on a switch but sees only darkness. Nonetheless, he moves toward the sink and begins to wash his face.

When he lifts his head, I am standing directly behind him, but only the top of my head and my eyes are visible over his own. The face rising over the back of his skull is one I have worn for many centuries, an oddity for one who has only seen sixteen years of life. But I have little cause to see myself in reflections, and sometimes I forget the face is mine.

Our gazes meet in the mirror, and the Stained Shirt Man shouts in alarm, stepping away. But when he turns back, all he sees is his own sweating face, drenched in water and fear.

Something gurgles

again.

This time, it is closer.

The Stained Shirt Man's eyes swing toward the bathtub. It is covered in dirt and grime and thin traces of bile. A large pool of blood is forming underneath it, spiraling outward until it touches the tips of his leather boots.

Tag,

the blood is saying.

You

are

it.

And from inside this bathtub a decomposing hand reaches out, grabbing the side with enough strength that the porcelain cracks from the urgency of its grip. The Stained Shirt Man slides to the floor in shock and fright, legs suddenly useless, as

I

heave myself up and over the side of the bathtub to land in

a heap of flesh before him. I am writhing. My body stiffens and contracts, tangled hair obscuring enough features that you would not know what I am, only what I am not.

I gurgle a third time.

The Stained Shirt Man crawls back into the living room swearing and screaming. In his fright, he stains his pants with his own excrement. He grabs at a phone, but the line is dead. Stumbling back onto his feet, he tries to feel his way through the dark, the sputtering light of the television set his only guide. He finds the door and tugs at it frantically, but it will not open.

"Help me! Oh God oh God…Help me!"

He begins to drive his shoulder against the wood, his efforts redoubling once he realizes

I

have followed him out of the bathroom, slithering, slithering, bone joints cracking and noisy from disuse.

"Shamrock!" His voice totters on panic. "Shamrock, can you hear me! Anybody out there! I…Jesus! Jesus Christ, help me!"

There is terrible contorting in the way the figure he sees moves. It does not crawl. It does not speak. There is only a dreadful, singular purpose in the way its fingers and feet scuttle closer, spread from its body like a human spider, though I am neither human nor spider.

The Stained Shirt Man soon realizes the futility and sinks back to the ground. "Was it the girl?" he asks then, and in his piggish eyes, dreadful realization seeps through. "Was it the girl? I didn't mean to…I never—I swear I won't do it again, I swear! I won't do it again!"

He is right. He will never do this again.

"Please," he croaks, lifting his hands as if they could shield him, and whether he is asking for mercy or wishes to be killed quicker, I do not know. "Please please please pleasepleasepleaseplease."

Something gurgles one last time, and it is above him. He looks up.

This is how the Stained Shirt Man now sees me.

He sees a woman on the ceiling.

Her gray feet are bare, settled against the beams.

She hangs down.

Her chin is jutted out, her head twisted to the side in a way that the only thing certain is her broken neck.

She wears a loose, white kimono spattered in mud and blood.

Her hair floats down, drifting past her face like a thinly veiled curtain, but this does not protect him from the

sight

of her eyes.

There are no whites in her eyes; they are an impenetrable, dilated black.

Her skin is a mottled patchwork of abuse and bone, some of it stripped from the edges of her mouth. And yet her mouth is hollow, curved into a perpetual scream, jaws too wide to be alive.

For a long moment we stare at each other—he, another girl's murderer, and I, another man's victim. Then my mouth widens further, and I

de

tach

myself from the ceiling to lunge, my unblinking eyes boring into his panicked, screaming face.

Some time later, the other girl comes to stand by my side. Silently, she holds out her arms, knowing what comes next. The braid around her wrist dissolves. At the same time, the rope on the dead man's arm shatters like it was made of glass.

She is free. She is smiling at me with her gap-toothed grin. When the dead are young and have once known love, they bring no malice. Something glows inside her, something that flares brighter and brighter until her features and form are swallowed up, obscured by that blessed warmth.

Yearly festivals of *chochin* were celebrated in my youth, paper lanterns lit to honor the dead during older, younger times. In dimmer recollections I remember grabbing at those delicate, fire-lit paper lanterns and the excitement that coursed through me as I held them aloft. I remember running along the riverbanks, watching dozens of *chochin* afloat on the water, bobbing and waving at me as I struggled to keep pace, until they drifted off into larger rivers, into places where I could not follow.

I remember straining to see the lanterns floating away, growing smaller until darkness enveloped the last. I imagine them in my memory like tiny fireflies hovering over the river's surface, ready to find their way into the world. Even then I found the word fitting, soothing.

Fireflies.

Fire

flies.

Fire, *fly.*

I remember my mother's voice, warm and vibrant before the sickness crept inside her. I remember her telling me how *chochin* bear the souls of those who have passed away. It is why we light these representations of their essences, she said, and float them in rivers—to allow the waters to return them to the world of the dead, where they belong.

The dead girl, like many other dead girls before her, resembles these *chochin*. When she begins to shine so very brightly, I take her gently in my hands, the soft heat suffusing my being with a sense of peace I am unaccustomed to. It is only for a few seconds. But when you have resigned yourself to an eternity filled with little else but longing, a few seconds is enough.

I release her soul outside the Stained Shirt Man's apartment. By then she is nothing more than a glowing ball of fire cradled against my withered form. I close my eyes, trying to absorb every bit of warmth I can take from her—to bring out and remember during other colder nights—before lifting my hands to the sky. Unbidden, she rises up, floating briefly above me as if granting benediction, before she continues to soar higher and higher like an autumn balloon, until she becomes another speck of cloud, another trick of the light.

Fire,

fly.

I am where dead children go. But not even I know where they go when I am done, whether to a higher plane or to a new life. I only know this: like the *chochin* of my youth, where they go, I cannot follow.

I stand there for a long time, just watching the sky. But nothing else moves in that darkness, and in this wide expanse of night, I see little else but stars.

CHAPTER TWO

THE TATTOOED BOY

The city wakes to the rhythm of daylight.

They first arrive in ones and twos. Lone boys with bicycles and newspapers, waging war against doorsteps. I count them: four, five, six. Men and women running down streets, singing aloud to music no one else hears. I count them: seventeen, eighteen, nineteen. A portly official thrusting important papers and packages into every other mailbox. I count him: one.

Then they arrive by the dozens. Men and women hurrying down sidewalks, a few in dark business suits, but the majority dressed simply in plaid or jeans. Some glance down at their wrists with an impatient air before boarding the horseless carriages they call buses or the smaller ones they call cars. (Twenty-seven.) Others saunter down the road with less urgency, with dogs of various breeds and sizes scampering ahead, restrained only by the collars around their necks. (Fourteen.)

A few dogs see me and growl, baring their teeth. I bare my own teeth and immediately they are off, tearing down the street in fright like hell has come nipping at their tails, their masters helpless in their pursuit. I have little regard for animals, and I imagine the feeling is mutual. Their leashes remind me of my own. Collars are as much a form of slavery whether they encircle necks or wrists, whether they are as heavy as lead or as light as a ropestring.

Finally, they come in droves. People in rich suits and richer tastes hurrying along, their minds immersed in the petty affairs that consume their lives (thirty-eight). Children squabbling in cars on their way to school, mothers and fathers behind the wheel (sixteen). They have no reason to see me—an unavenged spirit, a nothing-more. I am not a part of their world, as much as they are no longer a part of mine. They have the rest of their lives before them, and I do not.

I often spend the passage of days in a strange haze. When there is little to attract my vengeance, I lie in unusual states of hibernation.

Some days I curl up in attics and abandoned sheds. I do not sleep, so instead I exist in a period of dreamlessness, a series of finite instances where I think little of things and dwell on the wonders of nothing. It lasts for hours or days or years, or the time it takes for a bird to flap its wings, or the time it takes for a deep breath. But soon the rage curls again, the quiet places inside me that

whisper, whisper whispering find more find more

and so I rise, driven to seek out, to

devour, to make to break to take.

I have ridden on ships and sails. I have taken to the air on steel wings. I have schooled myself in the languages of those I hunt, their culture of contradictions. I have burrowed into the skins of those who know the dark ways, those who welcome the trespass of body. I have crawled out from the thickness of blood, from the salt of the dying.

I can possess, however briefly, those close to death, or those who have known death intimately and escaped. I have learned to move among people in a hundred different ways, to linger in numerous places at once and still keep my sense of being. But today I am drifting, aimless in this moment, basking in the afterglow of the night before.

And when there is nothing else, I count.

I allow the whim to carry me farther down the street, where a lone peddler sells food from a metal stand (one). A cat on the other side of the road (one) arches its back and hisses at me, yowling its temerity, though its tail quivers and the hairs along its back bristle. People walk past, eating and tossing empty wrappers into bins. I count them: thirteen, fourteen, fifteen.

A young man in a tan suit stops in mid-bite to stare directly at me. Slices of bread slide unnoticed to the ground, and he begins to tremble. I move, retreating as a group of students run past (seven), laughing and giggling, and flicker out of his vision. I am occasionally seen by those cursed with a peculiar sight they themselves are rarely aware of, but I have grown skilled at evading their scrutiny once discovered. I have no quarrel with the young man, who dashes away pale and frightened, though I am sorry he sees more than he ought.

But something else commands my awareness. It is a teenage boy in a car driving past this intersection of roads. He is of average countenance, perhaps fifteen years old, with bright blue eyes and straight black hair that shoots out unnaturally from his head like spikes. He is staring out the window with a surly demeanor I have found common in many boys of this time.

But neither his features nor his behavior arrest my attention. There is something that throbs and moves from inside his clothes, restless movements both repugnant and familiar. An unnatural glow sets around him. And in his mind I taste the sweetness of home, the land of my once-birth, thousands of miles away.

The boy does not notice all this. His eyes look out on the world and pass over me, unseeing, as the car turns a corner into a smaller lane.

It stops in front of a large house where several men are moving furniture out of a large truck that says "Picking's Movers" on its side. Tables and chairs and many more items litter the yard outside the house (sixteen). Some of these men (ten, a perfect number) are moving more in: two wooden beds, one vanity stand, sixteen assortments of electric devices, and many boxes. One mirror.

The boy gets out of the car, still scowling, with an older man of the same blue eyes, though his hair is a dirty yellow. They watch as the men move their furniture inside. I count the boxes: one, two.

"What do you think, Tark?" the older man finally asks.

The boy doesn't answer. Ten, eleven.

"It's nicer than our old house in Maine, don't you think?" the man continues, ignoring the silence. "You'll get your own room, of course—bigger, with more windows. We've got enough space to put up a rec room, maybe a swimming pool in the backyard once we're done settling in. It's only two blocks from Callie's place, too." Seventeen, eighteen.

Still the boy does not answer. He continues to watch the movers. The strange light persists around him, a queer dimness that radiates more than it shines.

"And we can go visit Mom next week. Dr. Aachman says she's been feeling a lot better than the last time, and that we can go to the hospital whenever we're ready. And now that we're only twenty minutes from Remney's, we can visit as often as you want." Twenty-five, twenty-six.

A peculiar shift crosses the boy's face, and I see emotion in him for the first time. The jaws tighten, the eyes harden, the mouth curves down. He folds his arms across his chest and a sleeve rides up, exposing a black tattoo on his forearm. Thirty-three boxes.

It is curious for a boy his age to possess tattoos of any kind.

Someone made a curious choice in the design of the tattoo on his arm. It is of two circles, the larger encompassing the smaller sphere and covered in meticulous writing, but of a language I do not understand. More symbols mark the length of his arms, climbing up to disappear, hiding under the folds of his shirt. These tattoos cause him to glow with that strange light as they hum and throb against his skin. As if suddenly aware of my scrutiny, he pulls the sleeve down.

"Dad, I'm not sure I should be visiting Mom at all," he says.

"Don't say that, Tark. I know she misses you."

"Trying to scratch my eyes out is a strange way of showing just how much she misses me." The bitterness is apparent in his voice.

"Dr. Aachman says that's not going to happen anymore," his father says firmly. "She'd been given the wrong kind of medication, that's all. We'll visit her right after your session with Miss Creswell on Wednesday. Okay?"

The boy only shrugs, though the anger in his eyes does not go away. Neither does the fear.

I pass into the house. Some of the inner rooms are bare, while the movers are gradually filling others with boxes and crates. I move upstairs into more empty rooms and, perhaps out of habit, drift to the ceiling. The previous owners left nothing of themselves here: no happiness, no grief, no pain. It is the best anyone can wish for in a place to stay.

Down below, the movers continue their work while the older man supervises. The boy sidles away to seek solace under the shade of a tree, shielding his eyes to glance up at this new house. Then his eyes widen.

"Hey! Hey, you!"

He runs into the house before anyone can stop him, and after trading startled looks with some of the movers, his father follows suit, confused by the boy's excitement, his sudden animation. By the time he catches up, the boy is standing by the window, unable to explain the room's emptiness.

"Didn't you see her? There was someone in here!"

"I don't see anyone, Tark," his father says after a pause.

"It was a woman!" The boy prowls the room, then moves into the next, still hunting for a presence and finding nothing. The father follows. "She had long hair, and she was dressed all in white!"

His father places a hand on his son's shoulder in a manner I believe is meant to offer comfort, but not belief. "It's been a long trip. Why not take a little nap in the car? I'll wake you up as soon as they get most of the things inside."

A pause, then the boy nods, having little of either evidence or alternatives. They walk back outside, but rather than getting in the car, the boy remains outside by the gardens. He continues to watch the house, seeking something to prove himself right and his father wrong. But I am careful, and he sees nothing but an empty house where spirits do not wander.

But someone else watches him. Another car is parked two houses away, a white one, small compared to the many others that roam these streets. Its driver observes the boy, and I know this because I can feel his hunger reaching out like a web of invisible malice. From the direction of this small, white car, I hear sounds of weeping, and I recognize these noises all too well.

I leave the house and steal across the street. I slip into the man's backseat and study him with the mirror that dangles over his dashboard. Unlike the Stained Shirt Man, he is clean-shaven and handsome. His suit is dark and very well-pressed. He has green eyes and brown hair. Other people might say he looks "friendly" and also "kindly" and "well-mannered." He is smiling, but there is nothing in his eyes.

There are dead children strapped to his back.

(One girl, two girls, three.)

They fill the car with cries and lamentations. I see the familiar pieces of rope on their wrists, all affixed to the man's forearms. But like the others, the smiling man takes no notice and continues to watch the tattooed boy.

(Four girls, five, six.)

They are blondes and redheads and brunettes. They are blue-eyed and dark-eyed and brown-eyed and green-eyed. They are pale and freckled, and dark and brown. They are six years old and eight years old and twelve years old and fifteen years old.

(Seven, eight, nine, ten, eleven.)

Some of these children have been tied to him for almost twenty years, others only since the month before.

(Twelve. One boy, two boys, three, four, five.)

He smiles now, this smiling man. It is how he sets his bait, how he entices. And his smile this time is for the boy with the tattoos.

I could take him

take take him take him

now. I could take his smiling, putrid little head and crush it

crush it crush

in my mouth. I could make him suffer. I could make him scream

scream scream scream SCREAM SCREAM

for me. Daylight holds no power over spirits such as me.

But I prefer the thrill of night. I prefer the same enclosed spaces in which these people do their work, where they feel themselves at their most powerful. It is a greater pleasure to kill in darker pastures, that much I know. It is not much of a vanity, but that is all that remains with me.

The Smiling Man

> *take him crush him*

starts his car. The dead children watch me as I watch him drive away, and I know I will see him again. I quell the hungers, the quiet places, and they retreat, for now.

The boy, too, intrigues me—for the first time in as long as I can remember—and that is a long, long time. His strange tattoos intrigue me. What lies moving underneath them intrigues me. There is something inside the boy that calls and repulses. There is something strange and malevolent hiding inside him, though I know not what, or why.

There is something inside him that reminds me of home.

I want to know the language of his strange tattoos. And time is one of the few things I have left to spend.

And when the Smiling Man

> *take him*

makes his move—as I know he will—I will be there. Waiting for him.

Until then, I can keep my own vigil.

For in this new house, there also is an attic.

CHAPTER THREE

LIGHT SHATTERS

Few things of note pass during the nights at this new house, despite what finds residence in the empty room upstairs.

The lethargy finds me again, and by the time I become aware, several days in the tattooed boy's lifetime must have passed. The furniture has been unwrapped and assembled, and the rooms no longer look abandoned. The man inspects the attic only once but quickly leaves again, unsure why he is repelled by its strange emptiness.

It is morning. The tattooed boy is sitting at a table, and his father is cooking, steam lifting from various metal pots and pans. The boy does not look happy. He is wearing dark pants and a long-sleeved shirt he keeps pulling down over his arms. The tattoos that so fascinate me only seem to anger him. He does his best to cover them up so no one else sees, though there is nobody present but his father, who has seen them many times.

"School blows," he says by way of greeting. I count the plates in the kitchen. Eleven.

The father sighs like he has heard this all before. "I know it's going to take some time for you to get used to a new city and a new school, Tark, but you have got to meet me halfway on this one. Applegate has a lot of friendly people. Even my boss is nice, which is about as rare a thing as you can imagine." He is attempting to be funny, but nobody laughs.

"Not really." The boy bites into his bread with admirable ferocity, tearing a good chunk of it out with his teeth. I count glasses. Six.

"I'm sure things will be better today," his father says encouragingly. The boy looks unconvinced and shrugs again. It appears to be his favorite habit. I count the spice racks that line the walls. Eight.

In the time it takes them to finish, I have counted the flower patterns on their wallpaper, the lights overhead, the knots in the ceiling, the kitchen tiles. I follow them into the car, where there is very little conversation. The tattooed boy fidgets uneasily on occasion and often glances over at his right, like something out of the corner of his eye puzzles him. But when he looks my way, all he sees is the window where other cars pass them by, swift glimpses of pedestrians, and other ordinary sights.

The car stops before a large building that says Perry Hills High. Beside it is another with a sign proclaiming it is Perry Hills Elementary. A series of corridors and walkways connect one to the other. A blond girl stands outside the main doors of the elementary school, a troubled look on her face. At eighteen, she is younger than she looks, though her manner and actions are those of an adult. Children stream past her to enter, but she ignores them, waving at both the boy and his father.

"Uncle Doug! Tark!" She is smiling, but the worry in her brown eyes does not match the curve of her mouth. "Tark, you're going to be late for class!"

The boy groans but accepts her hug willingly enough. "I'm not one of your fourth-graders, Callie."

"Sorry," the young woman says, not sounding sorry at all, "but that doesn't change the fact it's already two minutes to eight."

"Ah, crap. I'm out of here. See you later, Dad, Callie." He hitches his backpack, and a tattoo briefly slips out again from underneath his shirt as he turns to leave. The young woman sees it but is unsurprised, though the worry on her face grows.

"How's my favorite niece?" the man asks with a grin. "I must say—I expected the teachers here to be older. Why didn't you tell us you were working for the faculty?"

The young woman blushes. "I'm a teacher's assistant—not a full-fledged teacher yet. For now, I mostly get by with tutoring and babysitting, but Mom insisted on paying the rent 'til I leave for college next year."

"Good to hear. And speaking of Linda, how is she?"

"Mom's still with Doctors Without Borders. Still fighting malnutrition in Africa—and winning, if you believe the last email she sent me. She'll be back just in time for Christmas."

The young woman pauses, glancing behind her to ensure her cousin is out of earshot. "I'm worried about Tark," she says, lowering her voice as if fearful others might hear. "I didn't want to mention it in front of him. I had a feeling he was a little touchy on the subject. But it's those…those strange tattoos on his arms."

"I did my best to explain them to Mr. Kelsey, if that's what you mean," the man begins, but the young woman shakes her head adamantly, nervously tucking wisps of wheat-yellow hair behind her ear.

"All the principal told the other teachers—and all Mom told me, for that matter—was that his mother gave him those when he was only five years old. I never really knew Aunt Yoko, and I don't want to hurt Tark any further and pry, but—something about those tattoos scares me. A couple of times I've looked over at him, and I could have sworn…"

"Could have sworn what?"

That his tattoos were moving is what she wants to tell her uncle, but she does not. She does not tell him that the boy feels *wrong*. She does not tell him that she cannot shake off the feeling that there is someone else in the room, watching, when he is there. She does not tell her uncle because she believes it to be a figment of her imagination, a mockery of her senses. It is the permanent ink staining her cousin's skin, she tells herself, spreading across the canvas of her imagination. All these thoughts she keeps to herself and does not say aloud. What she says instead is this:

"I just want to know if I can do anything to help. He doesn't seem to want any friends, and he always keeps to himself. Nobody's been going out of their way to bully him or anything like that, but few people go out of their way to befriend him, either."

"Tark's been doing pretty well at home, considering," the man says. "He stays in his room a lot, but he doesn't listen to death metal or write about suicide or anything of that sort, thank God. Your cousin's a good kid. I don't want to pressure him into doing anything he's not comfortable with yet. And for the record—he wasn't abused by his mother. Not in the way you... He wasn't abused. It's a little complicated."

He tries to smile again. "Thank you for being concerned, Callie. I was worried you wanted to talk because his teachers told you Tark was being disruptive in class or getting into fights with the other students. He's been seeing a therapist, and he's still a little moody around other people, but he's improving."

The young woman nods. "Okay. I just—I just wanted to be sure."

"I would appreciate it if you could keep an eye on him whenever you can, though. Moving here was a little tough on Tark, and he could use a friend."

"Or an overbearingly fastidious older cousin to boss him into having a social life," the young woman finishes. The man laughs at this, but as he walks away after one last hug, I can see that his brows are drawn together and his eyes are tired.

After he leaves, the young woman stands there for a few more minutes until a bell rings and rouses her from her trance. She wraps both arms around herself and shivers before turning to enter, pulling the large doors closed behind her.

I spend the rest of the day counting. There are two janitors roaming the school grounds. There are sixteen rooms in the building. There are thirty students in the tattooed boy's class, and most ignore Tarquin in the same way Tarquin ignores them. Once, a girl beside him asks for notes from Mr. Spengler's history class from the day before, and he looks at her in a way that makes her uneasy. Still, she persists.

"Your name's Tarquin, right? That's an odd name."

"It's the name of some Roman emperor everyone's pretty much forgotten," the boy says, hoping she will take the hint.

She does not. "My name's Susan. Where are you from?"

"I'm from Texas," the boy lies. "Home to beloved exports like *The Texas Chainsaw Massacre*, mad cow disease, and bullets. I collect mannequin legs and spider bites. A race of super-ferrets live inside my hair. They hate water so I shower with an umbrella. I eat bugs because I'm allergic to fruit. I wash my hands in the toilet because sinks are too mainstream. Anything else you want to know about me?"

The girl gapes at him. Her friend nudges her away. "Just ignore him, Nat," the girl whispers. "He's weird."

Nobody else bothers him for the rest of his classes. The boy prefers it this way.

There are thirty-two students in one of the elementary-school classrooms next door. Of these thirty-two, one giggles when she spots me.

"Is there something funny you would like to share with the class, Sandra?" The teacher does not sound happy.

"There's a pretty girl at the back of the room, just standing there," the girl objects, pointing straight at me. It is the other students' turn to laugh.

"Don't make up stories, Sandra. Pay attention," the teacher says, and the girl obeys, though she cranes her head to look in my direction whenever the woman doesn't see, still grinning at me.

Soon the teacher leaves, and the yellow-haired, eighteen-year-old girl from before takes her place. As part of the lesson, she wheels in a large cart.

"Mrs. Donahue's still out on maternity leave, so it looks like you guys will be stuck with me for another week," she says with a grin. "I promised last time we'll be conducting our own experiments in static electricity, right?" The students sit up, interested.

The tattooed boy is done with his own classes for the day, and at that moment he is passing through the hallway, where he stops to watch his cousin at work. The young woman sees him and smiles, and the boy lifts a hand in greeting. She gestures at him to enter the classroom.

The little girl, Sandra, is the first to see the tattooed boy. The smile slowly slides off her face.

"This is my cousin, Tarquin Halloway. Say hi to Tarquin." A chorus of "Hi, Tarquin's" echoes around the classroom. "He'll be assisting me in this experiment." Tarquin shakes his head, waving his hands to show just how terrible he thinks the idea is. "Don't be shy, Tarquin. Class, would you like Tarquin to help out today?"

Another choruses of yeses from the class, and a whimpered "no" from the girl called Sandra, whom no one hears.

The boy does not know which is worse: social activity, however brief, or turning his cousin down and losing face in a classroom full of ten-year-olds. In the end, he sighs and opts for the former.

The young teacher brings out several lightbulbs and dozens of combs. The boy places his backpack on her desk.

"I've wrapped all the bulbs in transparent tape because I know some of you are all thumbs—yes, Bradley, that means you." More students laugh. "I don't have enough lightbulbs for everyone, but I do have enough combs, so I'll be dividing you all into groups of four."

The students troop up to take the lightbulbs from the cart, until only one remains on the teacher's table. The teacher's assistant gives each student a plain silver comb. "Now, we're going to need absolute darkness. Shut all the windows while I turn off the lights."

This is done promptly, and from inside the dark there are whispers and giggles, until a flashlight switches on. The young teacher sets it at the edge of the table, light trained up at the ceiling. I begin to count. One bulb, two.

"This is the best part. Bend your head my way, Tark." She picks up a comb and runs it briskly through Tarquin's hair. The boy looks resigned to his fate. The students giggle again.

"You can rub the comb against your sweater or anything fuzzy if you'd like, but make sure to do it for as long as you can and let it charge up." Some of the students copy her movements; others all but scrub their combs against their shirts, switching hands when the first one grows tired. Three, four.

"Ta-da!" the young woman says, and taps her comb against the lightbulb. There is a faint sputter, and inside the bulb, little lights begin to dance briefly at its center before winking out, like small handmade fireflies. Five, six.

There are several oohs and aahs, and more bulbs begin to spark and twitch around the room as students press their combs closer. Seven, eight.

Nine.

Nine

bulbs, all bearing strange little fireflies.

"That's how normal electricity works, too, but to a much greater extent, of course. Otherwise, you'll have to keep brushing your hair thousands of times just to watch a half-hour episode of your favorite show."

No

nines.

Not-nine,

Nevernine.

The girl named Sandra eyes me strangely.

"Whenever you do things like comb through dry hair, or wear socks and shuffle your feet along a really fuzzy carpet, you generate what's called static. Remember what we talked about last time, about electrons? One way to move electrons from one location to another is by—"

NO

     NINES!

The teacher's table rattles, like something has taken hold of its legs and is knocking them hard against the floor.

No nines

          no nines never

      nines NO

   NINES NO

           NINES

       NO NINES!

The lightbulb on the young woman's table ex

   plodes

without warning.

At the same time, the flashlight trained on the ceiling catches on a face there, a woman hanging upside down. Tarquin jumps back, mouth open.

There are gasps and cries of surprise, of fear. Somebody switches on the lights.

It is the young woman. She stares down at the misshapen bulb on her table, the glass irrevocably and inexplicably crushed, the tape still wrapped around what remains of its shape.

Though the air is warm, the tattooed boy is white and shivering, trying to pull more of his shirt around himself. The glow around him grows marked, and the tattoos hiding underneath his clothes ripple. It is almost like a shadow is rising out from them, snaking past his chest and neck.

"How—how—" The young teacher stutters, then remembers the sea of inquiring faces before her. She checks the ruined bulb hastily and seems relieved that none of the glass has flown out of the tape. "This is why you mustn't try this at home without any parental supervision," the young woman finishes, but it is clear that she herself is distressed over what has happened, though she fights hard not to let it show.

The boy's shivering has also passed. Color returns to his face, but he, too, is unnerved. The peculiar shadow seeking to fold itself around him has disappeared.

"Experiment's over for now! Who can tell me what the difference is between a positively charged atom and a negatively charged one? Brian?"

The lessons continue until the bell rings again and the children file out of the classroom, eager to be off. "I want everyone to leave the room through the back door!" the young woman warns. "Just to be on the safe side, in case there's glass on the floor that needs sweeping up!"

"I'm sorry," she tells the boy after most of the students have left. "I have no idea how that happened." The boy's backpack has fallen off the table, some of its contents spilling out: one binder, three books, and two sharpened pencils. The young woman bends to pick them up.

"Oh, these are good, Tark!" She holds up the binder, now

opened to pages of quick sketches and rough drawings: landscapes, animals, miscellaneous people.

The boy snatches it back. "Thanks," he says, more embarrassed than angry. He stuffs it back into his bag. "I really gotta go, Callie. There's a shrink waiting to see if I meet her minimum requirements of crazy."

"Stop that," the young woman says with a natural firmness that she often adopts with her charges. "You're not crazy, so stop saying you are."

The boy grins at her. Something unnatural lurks at the corner of his eyes, something not even he seems aware of. "Sometimes I wish I could believe that, Callie. But my own mother's batshit crazy, and I've seen so much other strange crap in my life that there's no doubt I'll be following in her footsteps soon enough." He glances up at the ceiling again, but there is nobody there. "I don't think your attempts at immersing me in the sanity of the general population's hive-mind are going to work here, but thanks anyway."

"Tark!" But the boy has already walked out of the room, a hand raised in farewell.

The young woman sighs, sinking into her chair. She picks up the broken bulb and turns it sideways. There is no doubt that the glass inside has been smashed, like a hammer has been violently taken to it. A shield of tape still holds some of the shards in place.

"What happened to you?" she whispers, her tone wondering. She lifts it to get a better view and sees her own slightly distorted image on the surface, tiny and unfocused.

As she watches, another reflection within the bulb moves beside her own.

She gasps, whirling around.

"Miss Starr?"

It is the girl called Sandra. The young teacher's heart is pounding. "Sandra! You startled me…"

"She's really sorry," the child says sincerely.

"Who is?"

"The girl who broke the lightbulb. I know she's sorry. It's 'cause you brought nine a' them. And she really, really doesn't like the number nine."

The young woman stares at her.

"I still like her better than the other lady, though."

"The other lady?"

"The lady with the strange face. The one with Mister Tarquin. She scares me."

She skips out, leaving the young woman staring after her, and on her face I can read her terror.

There is a crackling sound. Something is on the floor, trapped underneath a table leg. It is a piece of paper from the tattooed boy's binder.

The young woman picks this up with shaking hands. Unlike the other detailed drawings the boy has drawn, this is a mass of uneven loops and spirals. It is a rough drawing of a lady in black wearing a pale white mask, one half-hidden by her long, dark hair.

CHAPTER FOUR

BLACK AND WHITE

The therapist is named Melinda Creswell. That is the name written on a small golden plaque on the door: Melinda J. Creswell and, underneath that, Psychotherapist. Past the door is a room with two armchairs, two footrests, one couch, and one long table filled with folders. Two windows look out onto the busy street below. There are three certificates framed on the wall and one leafy plant in the corner.

The tattooed boy walks in with an air of expecting to be pounced on and devoured. He stares at a large painting of a summer meadow like he believes a wild beast is lying in wait for him amid the painted weeds.

Melinda Creswell herself is smaller than the room implies. She has graying curly hair and a rosebud mouth, and she is pouring tea the wrong way into two small, unadorned cups. She uses no bamboo whisks or caddies, and so the steam rising from the resulting mixture is of unsatisfactory sweetness. Finally, she smiles at him. "Hello, Tarquin. How was school today?"

The boy says nothing. He slumps into one armchair, and the

woman sits across from him in the other, offering a cup and a plate of small, round cookies that he halfheartedly accepts. I begin counting the books behind her, which fill numerous shelves spanning from one wall to the next.

"I've just had a talk with your father," the therapist says, "and I understand you've been having difficulty adjusting to Applegate since moving here. Do you want to talk about it?"

The boy blows noisily into his cup and takes a small sip. Then he sets the tea to one side.

"All right. Let's cut to the chase."

"What do you mean?"

"My dad paid you money to get me sitting in this chair— probably overpaid you, too, since his solution to every problem is to throw money in its face until it chokes from taxes. I'm pretty sure you have all my vital statistics—height, weight, eye color, allergies, my favorite breakfast cereal. You know we're from northern Maine, which is the coldest part of the United States except Alaska. There should be a government mandate preventing anyone other than yetis and hobbits from living in northern Maine, that's how cold I think it is.

"And now we're in Applegate, where the sun is actually doing its job but where the people are all so. Damn. Friendly. I can't take two steps without someone asking how I'm doing, or what my name is, or why I'm wearing thick clothes in this kind of weather, as if they're all required by the government to introduce themselves to everyone else like friendly, neighborhood child molesters.

"We're here because Dad found a bigger and better-paying white-collar job—you'd think he was the only investment banker up north the way he carries on—and so we could be closer to my mother, who is clearly crazy and who has on occasion declared her undying love for her only son by nearly strangling me to death. So yes, I am thrilled at the prospect of putting myself within spitting distance for her to try again. And the absolutely mind-blowing conclusion you've reached is that I may be having 'difficulty adjusting since moving to Applegate'? Really, Sherlock?"

The woman waits placidly until he is done with his spiel before speaking again. "Do you hate your mother, Tarquin?"

The boy looks back at her, and some of the anger leaves his face. "No. I've never hated her."

"Are you afraid of what she might do to you?"

"Only because what she does appears to be catching." A pause. "I killed someone, you know."

The therapist sounds calm and unworried despite this admission. "Who did you kill?"

"Some boy at school."

"Was he a friend?"

"Only if you're the kind of masochist that enjoys being beaten up by 'friends.'"

"I was told by your father that the police investigated what happened to you at your old school. They said there was no possible way that you were responsible for that."

"Still my fault he's dead." The boy shifts. "I really don't want to talk about it anymore."

"That's all right. I don't want you talking about anything that makes you uncomfortable. How about telling me something about your relatives here in Applegate, instead?"

"You mean Callie? She's great. She and Aunt Linda are the sanest and nicest people I know, which is another reason Dad decided to take the job and move here."

"I've heard she works as a teaching assistant at Perry Hills Elementary."

"It's something you'd expect someone like Callie to do. Callie loves kids. At least three times a year they visit us in Maine, despite weather that can freeze your toes off, and she never complains. We've always been close, for two people who live several hundred miles away from each other. She's like the big sister I never had. Callie's always taken care of me, even back then."

"How so?"

"She gets me out of trouble, for one thing."

"And are you often in trouble?"

"Got a knack for it. When I was six, I decided to eat crayons—I wanted to see if it would, uh, come out the other end in different colors, and my repeated failures made me all the more determined—and she made me barf them all out every time I did, before I could get sick. Another time I nearly sliced off my thumb making dinner, and she got me to a hospital before I was done hyperventilating. Little things like that." The boy smiles faintly at the memory. "I always joked that she was born old. She said it's because one of us had to grow up, and it wasn't likely to be me. I'd always been a stupid kid. Probably still am."

The boy pauses again. The woman is quick to pick up on the sudden change in his manner.

"Have you asked her for help recently?"

"Not...not recently, no. I decided not to."

"And why not?"

Again he hesitates. His eyes drift back to the painting. Ninety-eight, I count. Ninety-nine. One hundred.

"Because she won't believe me."

But the young woman has a strong capacity for belief.

"They're kids, Callie," her friend objects, a woman with short, black hair and a round face, nearly six years older. They are preparing to leave for the day, the school corridors empty of the students who swarmed out only hours before. "Of course they're going to say they see dead people. Didn't you watch the movie?"

The teenager is far from amused. "I'm serious, Jen. There's something strange going on."

"Sandra's one of my students, too, remember? She's always been a little spaced out. I don't think she's been weaned off imaginary friends yet. There's one of those in every class."

"No. I mean, yes, she's a little unusual, but I meant Tarquin."

"Your cousin, the Halloway boy? The one they say has all those tattoos on his arms? Poor kid. The one with the crazy mother? No offense," she adds quickly, but Callie shakes her head.

"I've never met Aunt Yoko. Uncle Doug told me it wasn't exactly abuse, but he didn't explain how it wasn't. It's not something they like talking about, and Mom always felt we shouldn't push."

"He'd say that, of course. Kid's got a hard enough life without having to advertise to the whole school that his ma's got several screws loose in the brain department. Have you seen them? The tattoos? He's always wearing those big shirts so I couldn't get much of a look. Not that I blame him for wanting to hide them."

"A few times, and always by accident. There are some small circles, right above his wrists, with very peculiar writing. I...I got chills just by looking at it. You know that cliché about the hairs standing up at the back of your neck? I feel that every time I see those tattoos, and I don't even know why. I have a feeling there are more of them he isn't showing."

"Have you asked Mr. Halloway anything more about them?"

"Where would I even begin? 'If you don't mind my asking, Uncle Doug, I'd like to know exactly how many tattoos Aunt Yoko gave Tarquin during her mental breakdown. Oh, no reason, they just scare the bejesus out of me.'"

"I think you're worrying too much about things that shouldn't be your problem, family or not. Know what my solution is? A boyfriend. I know this really cute guy a couple of years older than you. His name's Everett. Works part-time at the gym, planning on being a rocket scientist, literally. Aerospace engineering major. Has this sort of Jake Gyllenhaal vibe going…"

The blonde makes a face. "I'm serious, Jen. I don't like this."

"Neither do I, but we don't get to pick the kids they give us to teach, either, and we still have to like it. If we could, maybe I wouldn't have to read book reports that start: '*The Legend of Sleepy Hollow* begins when Johnny Depp goes into this weird town and gets chased by some guy with no head.'"

Both women laugh. "I have to go," the older one says. "Speaking of the hypothetically questionable upbringing of family members, I'm already running late. Jackson's working 'til eight, so it's my turn to pick Sean up from day care. I have no idea how they're both going to manage things here without me."

"So you're really set on going on that cultural studies program?"

"Absolutely!" Jen grins, excited. "Practically a month in France, all expenses paid—what's not to like? Well, most expenses paid. I don't think any planned shopping trips will count as research. Jackson's not happy about me not spending the summer here, but he agreed I shouldn't pass this up. You were accepted, too, weren't you?"

"I was—but I haven't decided on a country yet. Spain, Australia, India…they all sound tempting. I just feel a little guilty about leaving here before the school term officially ends."

"Well, it's not like a teacher's assistant is such a glamorous, well-paying job. Felicia Donahue's coming back in two weeks, anyway, so you won't have anything pressing to do. Think about going to

France with me, instead. Just imagine—reclining with cups of *café noisette* at a gorgeous little café, you being serenaded by a group of cute French boys while I'm waited on hand and foot by a charming waiter who looks suspiciously like Jean Reno…"

"Okay, okay, I'll at least *think* about it. Now stop daydreaming about inappropriately aged men and get out of here! Don't keep Sean waiting." The girl shoos away her friend, who walks on after one last wave. Only when she is finally out of sight does the teacher's assistant sigh, her face troubled.

It is then that she notices Sandra by the swings, singing softly to herself.

"And what makes you think she won't believe you?"

The boy snorts. "Some days I wish I didn't believe me, either."

"Would you like to tell me all about it?" the psychotherapist asks. The boy glares at her with a suspicious eye. One hundred and twelve, one hundred and thirteen.

"And what's going to stop you from putting me in the crazy bin if I do?" he accuses.

"I'll believe that it's something *you* believe," the woman says, and believes her own lie. "And if you're worried about me telling anyone else, I won't. Everything you say in this room will be strictly confidential. Not even your father has to know. The only reason for me to divulge information to anyone is if I have reason to believe that you are a danger to yourself or to the community, and I believe you are not a threat."

The boy considers this for a few minutes, then laughs. It is not a humorous sound.

"Sometimes when I look in mirrors, I see a strange lady."

To her credit, the woman does not blink.

"She's in a black dress, and she wears a mask. All she does is watch me, and not with that I've-got-a-crush-on-you kind of stare. Less infatuated, more homicidal. I always get this feeling like she's waiting for something, but I don't know what that is. She pops up in places I don't expect—mirrors, usually. She's fond of mirrors, unfortunately. If that makes me crazy, then you better have a strait-jacket ready, because that's the truth."

"I see." The woman's voice does not change. She picks up her cup again. "How long have you been seeing this lady?"

"I don't know. For as long as I can remember, I guess. Maybe since I was five, six years old. Sometimes I don't see her for months at a time, but now I see her almost every day, especially after moving here. It's—have you ever had the sensation of feeling eyes looking at you, except you know they're not really eyes?"

Even the woman's detachedness hesitates at such a description. "And you've never told anyone about this?"

"Dad's got some fuzzy notion about what's been getting my goat, but he doesn't believe me. He never does. He thinks I'm imagining things. It's hard to talk to him about anything, really." The boy's tone is surly. One hundred and twenty-eight, one hundred and twenty-nine.

"Has anyone else ever seen her?"

"I'm not sure. I don't think so."

"What about Callie?"

"Sometimes Callie looks at me funny, like she knows there's something wrong. But she's never said anything. And I don't want her knowing, anyway. Whatever this is, I want her out of it."

"Hello, Sandra," the teacher's assistant says.

The girl smiles back at her but says nothing. The young woman takes the swing beside hers.

"I was wondering about this woman you told me about. The woman standing behind Tarquin."

"Oh, that woman," the girl says. She stops swinging. "The lady with the funny mask."

"A mask?"

"I thought it was a face at first, but it's not. It has holes instead of eyes."

"Why don't you like her?"

"Because she's in prison. And she's been trying to get out."

This does not make much sense to the young teacher, so she tries again. "When did you first see this woman?"

"When Mister Tarquin came to class. He doesn't like her, either."

"Why don't you like her?"

"Because she wants to hurt Mister Tarquin. She wants to hurt me. She wants to hurt everybody. Except she can't. Not while she's still in prison."

"Sandra," the young woman says. She pauses, trying to frame the question right. "Sandra, where is this prison?"

Bright green eyes look back at her. "Mister Tarquin," the girl says. "Mister Tarquin's the prison."

"Let's talk a little bit about when you were younger, Tarquin," the therapist says. "What do you remember about your childhood?"

"Not a lot. Dad used to tell me stories about when I was little, though. Like I once nearly fell into a manhole, and I used to have a pet dog named Scruffy. But I don't remember anything. It's like the stories happened to someone else, not to me. You'd think I would have at least remembered the dog."

"What is the earliest memory you can recall?"

Another pause. "My mother," the boy says, and his voice is quiet and vulnerable. "I remember that she used to sing to me before I went to sleep."

"Was it a lullaby?"

"I don't know the song's name." The boy hums a little, and the melody is a strange, haunting one. One hundred and forty-three, one hundred and forty-four.

"I'm afraid I'm not quite familiar with that song," says the woman who specializes in caring for children and knows exactly one hundred and thirty different lullabies in her head.

"It's the first thing that I really remember," the boy said. "And then my mom had to... Well, she went bonkers, excuse the political correctness. Dad had her checked into Remney's. And shortly after they took her away, I started seeing that...that."

"I see," the therapist says. This, too, is a lie; she does not truly see.

"Your son is an exceptionally bright boy," she tells his father later, once the session is over. The boy is leafing through a small stack of magazines while the man and the therapist conduct a hushed conversation behind the door. "Much more intelligent than an average teenager his age, but he tends to express this through sarcasm and self-deprecation. It's a better outlet than other forms of rebelling I know of, but still not something I would like to encourage. He also suffers from a very deep-seated psychosis, very similar to post-traumatic stress disorder."

"Was it because of the McKinley boy's death?" his father asks, troubled.

"It doesn't seem likely. His hallucinations have nothing to do with any kind of flashbacks from the incident, which I find puzzling. I believe this may stem from feelings of abandonment caused by his mother leaving, though his symptoms are still quite peculiar. He exhibits no aggressive behaviors, as far as I can determine."

"Will he be all right?" the man asks.

"I'm not comfortable with administering strong antidepressants to someone so young. I suggest that he comes back for several more sessions so I can monitor his progress and let you know of any improvements. I recommend not putting him in any more stressful situations than he's already in."

"We're going to be visiting his mother in an hour's time."

The therapist frowns. "I'm not sure that would be healthy at this stage, Mr. Halloway, especially after the last time…"

"His mother's been asking for him," the father insists. "And I know that whatever he says, he misses his mother and wants to see her, too. We're taking very careful steps this time. Nothing is going to happen."

The therapist looks reluctant, but the father is resolute. The boy abandons the magazines, staring instead at a lone mirror on the wall.

"What about the other woman you mentioned?"

"She wears a white dress, not like the lady in black. It's really dirty, but that isn't her fault. Not really."

"Does she stand behind Tarquin, too?"

"Nope. She likes to stand upside down on the ceiling sometimes."

The young woman feels a decided chill. "How do you know all these things, Sandra?"

"I don't know," the girl says, puzzled herself. "I just see them, and then I do."

"Why doesn't she like the number nine?"

"She had ten things a long time ago, but then she lost one of them so now she only has nine, and she got hurt because of it. She doesn't like being reminded."

"Why does she like standing on the ceiling?"

"Sometimes she stands the right way like us, but she got used to ceilings, too. Someone hurt her really, really badly, and they put her down someplace that was dark and smelly, like a big hole. Her head went in the hole first before her feet and she died like that, so she got used to seeing everything upside down."

"I don't understand."

The girl swivels in her swing seat. She grasps the sides of the swing with both hands and tips herself over backward so that her hair grazes the ground and she is looking over at the teaching assistant from the wrong way up.

"Like this," she says. "She died looking at everything like this."

The father and the boy finally leave, and the therapist returns to the solitude of her office, back to the one hundred and sixty-three volumes on her bookcase. She picks up the small device she uses to record conversations with patients and presses a few buttons.

"My mother." The boy's voice comes from it, low and tinny. "I remember that she used to sing to me before I went to sleep."

"Was it a lullaby?" she hears her own voice ask.

"I don't know the song's name." The boy begins to hum.

Within the tape, something else begins humming in light counterpoint.

The therapist gasps and shuts the recorder quickly. She hesitates, steeling herself, and switches it on again. The boy's humming continues, but this time there is no other accompaniment.

Melinda Creswell, psychotherapist, looks around the empty room with growing unease, but by then I am long gone.

CHAPTER FIVE

MADWOMAN

The boy and his father enter a different building next, this one a dollhouse of white decay. The walls and floors are white. The doors are painted white and the ceiling is painted white and the windows are painted white, and whenever there are curtains, they are also white.

There are two kinds of dolls here. The first kind wears white shirts and pants. They hurry down corridors pushing white carts and carrying white towels, stacks of white paper, and white trays. They carry about themselves an air of forced joviality, though they know very well there are few things to smile about in these halls.

And then there are the broken dolls. They are pushed around in wheelchairs and fed, drooling, from plastic cups. Sometimes they are dragged, fighting and screaming, by the White Shirts into white beds inside white rooms. Needles are jabbed into their arms to keep them calm, but they are never truly cured. The broken dolls cry and laugh and shout and sing, and often they sound much more alive than the White Shirts.

The boy and his father follow one of the White Shirts down a long corridor where many broken dolls live. One doll is banging her head repeatedly against the wall, over and over, until another White Shirt comes to take her away. Another has soiled himself, a stream running down his leg even as he meows and swipes at his own head with a curled arm, oblivious.

Still another steps out of her room and sees them. "I curse thee!" she shrieks, lifting a spindly finger to point at a spot behind the boy. "I curse thee, foul abomination! In the name of the Father and the Son and the Holy Ghost, I abjure thee! Begone, foul spirit, begone, begone, begone!"

A Shirt takes her arm but she shakes him off, still spewing curses at nothing. More arrive, seven in all, to subdue the little woman, and she fights madly, like a crazed tiger struggling with its last breath to hurt one last time. "I abjure thee!" she wails. "For I am the Sword of God, and I order you to be gone, demon, begone begone begonebegonebegone—!"

She is dragged into another room, but the screaming continues.

The boy is unsettled, and so is the father, though he tries to hide it. "I'm sorry," the White Shirt tells them apologetically. "That's Wilma. She's been quiet the last several weeks. I don't know what's come over her today."

"What's wrong with her?" the father asks.

"She thinks she's the archangel Gabriel."

"Who was she talking to?" But the Shirt only shrugs, because it is not their job to know, only to help.

The room they seek is located at the end of the hall, on the far left. "We set up some Japanese sliding doors in her room, like you asked," the Shirt says. "She seems to like it, and she's been considerably calmer since they were installed. Says it reminds her of home." He pauses, shooting the tattooed boy a significant look. "She's under a heavy dose of medication right now, but I'm not sure she should see you just yet. You'll have to stay behind the screen until we're sure she won't react as badly as she did before."

The boy nods, though reluctant about this suggestion. The father squeezes his arm. The Shirt knocks quietly at the door.

"Looks who's come to visit again, Mrs. Halloway."

Inside, a woman sits on a white lounge chair. She is a beautiful lady: no longer youthful, but far from the old age the white streaks peppering her long, black hair imply. Her brown eyes are unfocused. In contrast to the whiteness of the dollhouse, a wooden shoji screen splits the room in half and prevents her from seeing those who stand beyond the door. But the screen is not what makes this room different from all the others in this building.

Unlike the people outside, the dolls filling this room are real. They occupy rows of wooden stands that mark every wall. A large platform stands beside the woman's bed, covered in heavy red carpeting, where a set of dolls have been carefully arranged—a likeness of the Japanese imperial family and their court, presiding over a roomful of subjects.

The dolls that surround the walls are of a different design. While the imperial dolls are smaller and more triangular in shape, the others are carefully proportioned *ichimatsu* dolls with faces that might at times pass for real children, if not for their affected stillness. Despite these differences, all the dolls in the room bear milky, porcelain-white skin. They are dressed in heavy robes and kimonos, colorful ornaments woven into their hair. Their eyes are colorless. All gaze down at the visitors with expressionless faces, draped in the silence that often comes before the passing of judgment.

"Who is it?" the woman asks. Though her smile is genuine, her words are slow to come, thick with unnatural lethargy. One doll, two dolls, three.

"Yoko?" At the Shirt's nod, the father enters the room. He slides part of the shoji to one side so he can step in and kneel by the woman. He is used to the presence of these dolls and thinks little of them, but the boy is not yet acclimatized. He does not follow, remaining hidden behind the partition. His eyes wander from doll face to doll face with nervous misgiving.

The man takes the woman's hand in his. "It's me, Yoko," he says gently, and all the love and worry are in his eyes. "It's Doug."

"Doug," the woman repeats. She smiles warmly at him. "It's been so long since you last visited, *anata*. I was so worried something had happened. It's been…It's been…" She falters, unable to remember. Nineteen dolls, twenty dolls, twenty-one.

"We'll be visiting more often," the man promises. "And Tarquin is here," he adds, though he now says this slowly and deliberately, watching her face anxiously for any signs of distress. The boy standing behind the screen waits, his back rigid. From his position, all he can see of his mother is her shadow, stooping behind the screen.

"Tarquin's here?" the woman says, this time with more animation. "Where is he?"

"Hey, Mom," the boy says. His voice is low, trembling with pent-up emotion. Gone is his usual derision, all traces of sarcasm lacking from his tone. For now, Tarquin Halloway is a fifteen-year-old boy who, for all he has endured, still misses his mother. For all his hurt, there is much forgiveness in him.

"Tarquin? Where are you?" The woman twists her head and moves as if to stand.

"He's here, Yoko," the man says, "but the doctors say you can't see him today." Forty-one dolls, forty-two dolls, forty-three.

"Did I hurt him?" Terror rings in her voice. "Did I hurt him again? I am so sorry, Tarquin, I am so sorry!"

Overwhelmed, she starts to sob. The man wraps his arms around her. The boy can only watch their shadows, helpless.

"It was the only way," the broken woman whispers. "I didn't know what else I could do. I didn't have much choice. But I couldn't let her out. Don't you see? I couldn't let her out!"

The White Shirt steps forward, alarmed, but the woman quickly rights herself, shaking off her ramblings. The sudden queerness in the air that had settled around her like dense fog is gone. She sits up straighter in her chair, now prim and delicate, though her hands twist and clench without her knowledge at invisible paper she is slowly tearing to shreds. Sixty dolls, sixty-one dolls, sixty-two.

"It was very nice of you to visit, Doug," she says calmly with no trace of her previous hysteria. "It's been so long since I last stepped out of these walls that I'd almost forgotten what it feels like to be outside."

"Yes," the man says, at a loss at how to respond.

"I'd like to go back to Japan again," the woman says, and her voice sounds like it is coming from somewhere else, far away. "It's been so many years since I've been back in Tokyo. I miss *hanami* in the springtime. Do you remember, Doug? All those times we would camp out underneath the trees and watch the cherry blossoms bloom 'til nightfall. How long has it been?"

"It's been seventeen years since we graduated from the University of Tokyo, Yoko." The man's voice is choked.

"Has it been that long since our *Todai* days? How odd. I still remember them as clearly as if they were only a week ago. I remember the *hanami* well." She laughs. "We had to look at six different shops just to find a *yukata* in your size."

"You always insisted on doing things the traditional way," the man said, smiling at their memories. Eight-five dolls, eighty-six dolls, eighty-seven.

"For *hanami*, it is only proper to dress in the right manner." She squeezes his hand. "The old ways of watching are always the best. Cherry blossoms die as quickly as they bloom, so one must always come with the proper clothes and the proper attitude to admire their beauty before they pass away so quickly. The great writer Motojirou-san said it best: '*Sakura no ki no shita ni wa shitai ga umatte iru.*'"

Dead bodies lie under the cherry tree.

The woman whips her head to stare at me, as if I had spoken the words out loud. Her face turns white, her eyes staring.

"Who's there?" she whispers, growing more agitated by the second. The man reaches out to take her hand again, but she shakes him free.

"Who's there?" She jumps out of her chair and begins to advance toward me, unexpected anger bleeding from every pore in her body. "There is someone in here! You! Who are you?" Her voice grows louder until she is all but screaming.

"Who are you?"

The White Shirt starts forward, intent on restraining her, should it become necessary, but there is strength in the woman still. The drugs that cloud her vision prove to be his undoing. She pushes him away, harder than it would seem possible, given her small frame, and the White Shirt crashes into the shoji screen, knocking it over and revealing the tattooed boy standing behind it, stunned and shaken by his mother's rage.

The woman sees her son, and then she begins to scream.

It is a howling symphony of loss and fear and madness. She leaps toward him, her eyes blazing and her hands clawed, transforming that pale, pretty face into that of a creature of malevolence.

"You!" she howls. "I will not let you escape! You will not have him! I will not let you have him! I'll kill him first! I'll kill him!"

At the same time, I see that aimless shadow drift up from behind the boy's stricken form, the same darkness I saw in the classroom that day, though there is more to its shape. Something is rising out of the boy's back—something with terrible, burning eyes, yet not quite eyes at all, preserved behind a bloodless, decaying mask that hides its face from the world.

Our gazes

meet.

The woman is still screaming, hurling vile curses into her stunned son's face. She fights off her husband's attempts to restrain her. "Get away from him! I will never let you out! I'll kill him first! I'll kill him I'll kill him I'll kill him!—" She stops only to reel off sutras and chant at breakneck speed in a language that should be familiar to me but is not, a language that crackles in the air, which now grows uncomfortably hot from the heat of her words.

The door flies open and several more White Shirts run in. With efficient precision, they surround the woman, cutting off her chants. She lashes out with her legs and her fingernails, dislodging dolls from their shelves in the process, but the Shirts are successful at incapacitating her, holding her long enough to jab a large needle into her arm. In time her struggles grow weaker until she finally sinks, exhausted, against a White Shirt's chest, her head nodding as she spirals into sleep.

"I'm sorry," a White Shirt tells the man and his son. "She'd been responding well to the lorazepam. I'm not sure what triggered this outburst."

"That's okay," the father replies. The boy says nothing, though his face is as white as those of the dolls that surround him. The dark fog has disappeared.

"I'm so sorry you both had to see this. But I think it would be best if we cut this visit short and give her more time to rest." The man nods and gently ushers his son out of the room.

With one final effort, the woman's eyes fly open. She lifts her head over the sea of White Shirts attending to her and stares directly at me. In her eyes there is desperation but also a sudden realization of my purpose here in this room of one hundred and eight dolls.

"I am so sorry," she whispers, imploring. "Please. Please protect him. Please…" The words trail off. Her head lolls to one side and her eyes fall shut. Within seconds, the drugs have taken their toll, and she is fast asleep.

The boy is frightened. He keeps glancing back at his unconscious mother, who is now being lifted by one of the bigger White Shirts onto her small bed.

"What did she mean?" he asks. His father looks at him. "Was she talking about me? Who was she talking to?"

"Your mother isn't well, Tark," the man tells him. "You shouldn't take to heart anything she says while she's in this condition. We just came at a bad time."

"We always come at a bad time!" the boy responds with violence in his voice. "What is it about me that she hates so much, that she can't even stand the sight of me?"

"Tark…I…"

"Forget it. Just forget it. I'm getting out of here." The boy brushes past his father and tears down the hall. Several of the patients jeer and cheer him on as he runs by, but the boy does not pay attention.

"Tarquin!" His father takes off after him. A woman reading a newspaper on a nearby bench lowers it to stare at the retreating visitors and then at me.

"Mad people," she observes sagely. "They're all mad."

Then she grins to show off rotting teeth, and she winks at me. "Not like us, dearie," she coos. "Never like us."

CHAPTER SIX

THE MURDER

This little town is not known for its displays of violence, and so the murder takes them by surprise.

It starts with the man who trudges into the block of apartments that litter the side of one street with gray. The man pauses by door 6A and pounds on the frame like he expects the wood to fall away from the force of his fists alone.

"Hey, Mosses!" he roars. "Mosses, open the fuckin' door and give me my money, you sonofabitch!"

If there is anyone alive inside, they do not answer. The knocking grows furious, violent.

"That's it, you fuckin' bastard! I want you the hell out of my place! I don't fucking care if you gotta sleep in the gutters tonight!" He yanks out a set of keys and fits one into the lock. He twists the doorknob and all but kicks the door open.

The rumors spread: first like tiny ripples, then growing until they overlap into wider spirals of gossip.

The first thing that people are told is that "there is a dead man in the Holly Oaks apartments."

The second thing they will be told is that "his face is bloated, like he was held underwater for a very long time." And yet there is not a drop of water on or around him, nothing to suggest foul play other than the appearance he presents. That is why the apartment manager, whose name is Shamrock, throws up all over the stair banister in his fruitless bid to escape the room and his first sight of the body, spattering an unfortunate couple standing below.

The police come next. They park their sirens in front of the building and mark off the area with yellow tape. "You can't go in there," one policewoman says to passersby and curious onlookers, as the other officers cordon off the scene. "This is a crime scene." They turn down interviews by reporters. "We cannot divulge anything more specific until after a full investigation has taken place."

Some of the reporters showed up before the police arrived. "This is Cynthia Silvia from WTV Channel 6," one reporter tells the camera and the world watching through the lens. I count them—the police, the growing number of people. I drift past the camera and peer into the frame, though no one notices. "Very little information has been released so far, though the police believe this to be a homicide by a person or persons unknown. We'll update you as soon as we know more…"

"A thirty-five-year-old man was found dead in his apartment this morning. Sources tell us he may have been dead for days, though the police have yet to release any information corroborating this…"

"This marks the first homicide case in Applegate in almost ten years. Not much is known about the victim, thirty-five-year-old Blake

Mosses. He was a loner, according to his neighbors, and lived in Holly Oaks for only six months before his body was found…"

"This is Cooper Wilkes of ANTV Channel 5 News, reporting live from Holly Oaks…"

"This is Tracy Palmeri, Channel 2 News. Back to you, Jeff."

It would surprise these reporters to know that few stories begin with death. Often, they start with grief.

This story starts hundreds of miles away, where a small town in South Carolina gathers to pray for a young girl who has been missing for four months and who will never return home, although they do not realize it. Posters of her decorate every inch of tree and wall, and her sweet, gap-toothed smile enchants those who care enough to take a cursory glance. Her parents, a listless bearded man and a weeping woman, clasp hands as they implore the public to help in the search, knowing that in time their daughter will slip through their fingers and disappear into the archives of unexplained cases and old news.

The reports are different here from at Holly Oaks.

"Officers from two counties are continuing the search for eleven-year-old Madeleine Lindgren, who disappeared in May. Police have set up an AMBER Alert for the missing girl, and so far, thousands of tips have come through the hotline…"

"The police say they are going through every piece of information that passes through the channels but admit that, with the number of tips coming in everyday, filtering through the information will take time. More than a hundred officers and volunteers have joined in the search for little Madeleine…"

"If you have any information related to this case, please call the following numbers: 242-45…"

Strings of a story move through states and cities, leaving parts of the story at every stop. People find themselves at the beginning of a tale without an end, or in a middle that neither starts nor finishes, or at a conclusion that knows no beginning. Only two have read this story in its entirety, can quote it from cover to cover, and had been there from introduction to curtain fall.

One is the Stained Shirt Man that people are now calling Blake Mosses.

I am the other.

And when the news provides no other answers, gossip takes center stage.

For the neighbors at Holly Oaks apartments, it is their moment to shine. "Always knew he was a bad seed," says Greta Grunberg from 6D, who said no such thing to anyone until after the fact. "Skulking up and down the stairs, never leaving the room for days. He was going to come to a bad end, I always thought."

Annabelle Mirellin from 5C believes that Mosses was attacked by a wild animal and wonders if this could be possible grounds for suing Holly Oaks for mismanagement. She is not swayed from this belief by the fact that the door was locked from the inside and no trace of a wild animal was found inside the room.

The police, more sensible creatures than the neighbors, are baffled. But it will be days before they discover the small strand of hair hidden underneath the dislodged carpet, and it will be months before they fully understand its importance.

The Smiling Man is unconcerned about this most recent development. The town of Applegate is already proving to be a distraction, and he is busy planning, plotting his next move.

He parks his white car at one corner of the street and strolls toward where the crowd of people (fifty-seven) have gathered, watching in fascination as medical personnel (four) wheel out a large gurney that carries something (one) large and bulky, hidden from view by a large, black blanket. Many have never seen this manner of death up close, one that does not point the blame at old age or sickness.

This provides ghoulish enjoyment, for the town is too large to know of the little perversions that move in villages, yet too small for its residents' spirits to have been toughened by the crimes of cities. There is a thrill in relishing the suffering of strangers, and they hide their interest with worried faces. The dead man, Blake Mosses, had not been One of Them, and they can afford to treat him as a source of unfortunate entertainment rather than one of genuine bereavement.

The Smiling Man wanders in and out of the crowd, the dead children forced to keep up with every step. He does not bother to look at the man's corpse, for he does not specialize in this kind of death. His eyes are trained on a young girl who has wandered some distance away from the group. She sits on a small park bench opposite the apartment block, engrossed in her music.

The Smiling Man sets up shop at the other end of the bench, ostensibly to watch the drama unfolding on the other side of the street. He observes her when she is not looking.

"I don't think your mother would want you watching all this," he says after considerable time has passed.

The girl shoots him a suspicious look. Few adults, in her experience, would condescend to talk to children the way this man does with such impunity. She takes an earbud out of one ear. "Mommy's a policewoman," she says. "We were driving home from school when the alert came on her radio. She was the closest to the crime scene, so she had to investigate. Mommy says we don't have enough cops in this town, so we always have to adapt. She told me to stay inside the car," she adds, as if this was a trivial detail not worth repeating. "But it was stuffy inside."

"That is true," says the Smiling Man, whose interest wanes slightly once the girl divulges her mother's occupation. "But I don't think she'd like to hear you've been talking to strangers, either."

"Mommy said talking to strangers is dangerous," the girl admits. "Are you a stranger?"

"I live in Massachusetts," says the Smiling Man. "So I suppose you can call me a stranger. Can you say Massachusetts?"

"Massachusetts," says the girl. "I'm not an idiot. Are you dangerous?"

The Smiling Man laughs at her courage. "Well, it was dangerous for that man over there, wasn't it?" he asks, sidestepping her question and pointing toward the crime scene, where the crowd surges closer, straining to see more of the dead man as the medical technicians begin loading the body into the back of an ambulance. A flock of reporters (eight) swarm around the police officers (five), firing volleys of questions into the air at them like bullets. "They say he was a stranger, too."

"That's true," the girl concedes. "Maybe strangers can also be dangerous to each other."

The man laughs again, amused. "My name is Quintilian."

"Sandra," the girl counters and adds, "That's a weird name."

"My mother named me after a Greek philosopher."

"Mommy named me after her favorite soap-opera actress."

"Sandra is a nice name."

"I wish she'd named me after someone more famous. Like Marie Curie. I think Marie is a nice name. Or maybe Marie Antoinette."

"Marie Antoinette had her head chopped off by a group of angry Frenchmen."

The girl is unfazed by his choice of words. "But she got to go to parties and wear wigs and eat a lot of cake. What are the names of all your other friends?"

"What friends?"

"All those kids sitting on your back."

The man stills suddenly, and his smiling face changes. His gaze is now wary, and his hand slowly dips into his coat pocket and stays there. "There aren't any kids on my back," he says, trying to sound like a patient adult dealing with a rather precocious child.

"I can see them. They're grouped all around you, and they don't look very healthy. Why are they all afraid of you?"

"What an interesting child you are, Sandra," the Smiling Man says. "What a funny little child." From his pocket he withdraws a folded handkerchief, sending a faint whiff of chloroform into the air. He should not be doing this so close to the police cars, he knows, but sometimes the thrill of it fuels his motivations.

"You're quite creative when it comes to making things up, aren't you?"

"Sandra!" a woman's voice calls from where the throng of people is thickest, laced with a mother's worry and panic. "Sandra! Where are you?"

This produces a most unusual change in the Smiling Man. Where his body had been tense and coiled, as if he was biding his time to spring, he now relaxes and slides back against the bench. His hand slackens, and he slips the handkerchief he is toying with back into his pocket, out of sight.

"It appears your mother is looking for you, Sandra."

The girl pops the bud back into her ear and skips across to where her mother stands, a tall woman with cropped hair and a dark blue police uniform, a tall woman struggling between a job that takes up too much of her life and a child who needs too much of her time. The anxiety in her face shifts into a cross between welcome relief and anger as she spots her daughter.

"What did I tell you about leaving the car? I told you to stay inside!" she scolds, as she brings the girl to where a police car is parked half a block away, the windows rolled down and the doors unlocked.

"I'm sorry, Mommy," the girl says sincerely. "But it was really hot inside."

"What am I supposed to do with you, Sandra?" The woman is exasperated. This is not the first time her daughter has wandered off on her own.

"The guy from Massachusetts and all those kids with him kept me company."

"What guy from Massachusetts?" The woman's maternal instincts have been triggered, knowing there is something odd about her daughter's words without knowing why. She scans the crowd, hunting for a face that may strike her as strange or unusual.

But when her eyes come to rest on the bench, no one is sitting there. Making his escape while the cameras flash and the sirens turn on, while the door slams shut behind what is left of Blake Mosses and the ambulance speeds away, the Smiling Man has disappeared, and with him, all the dead children he has killed.

CHAPTER SEVEN

BREAD CRUMBS

Four days after the murder hits the front-page news, the manner and reasons for the stranger's death remain a mystery to the people of Applegate. The police have no suspects, and the bizarreness of the crime ensures that reporters are still quick to trot it out on evenings when the news is slow, though few updates warrant reporting.

People have taken to locking their doors or moving about their houses to check for open windows or stray curtains at night. They take the time to warn their children to come home before it grows too dark, cautioning them about the perils of nightfall, and they frequently look over their shoulders, waiting to hear the tread of steps behind them, expecting to observe and question every shadow that moves across the street.

Teenagers find death easier to deal with than adults do, and the news passes easily enough from their minds. Classes give way to lunchtime, and the cafeteria seats are occupied. There are the sounds of boys and girls laughing and gossiping as they congregate in groups and friendship.

The tattooed boy shares in none of the revelries, instead retiring to a corner of the cafeteria alone. Chewing on a sandwich, he stares at the wall across from his seat. He wears another long sweater and has resumed his habit of tugging his sleeves down until they reach well below his knuckles. The sun is shining outside and the air-conditioning is marginal at best inside, but he is huddled, quivering, and with every breath, tendrils of cold air billow out of his mouth. His eyes are dull.

"Hey there, stranger," a voice says. It comes from a pretty brunette his age who has a fresh face with a slight abundance of freckles and a penchant for friendliness. Her manner suggests that she is one of the more popular girls at Perry Hills High, and this means she is free to do as she pleases. Today what she pleases to do is to strike up the boy's acquaintance. Rumors of the tattooed boy have spread, and ironically, the boy's disinterest in his fellow students makes him more enigmatic and appealing in their eyes. "You must be this strange Tarquin fella some of the guys have been talking about. Wanna eat with us?"

"No," says the boy, who has a penchant for surliness.

The boy's yellow-haired cousin enters the cafeteria. She looks up, sensing by some obscure instinct that something is about to happen, and glances toward where the boy sits.

"Why not?" insists the brunette, who is not accustomed to being rejected. She reaches out and tugs playfully at the boy's hand, a show of coyness. "My name's Andrea. Come on, I don't bite."

"I said *no*." The boy tries to shake her hand off, but it is too late.

The dark-haired girl's fingers snag against his shirtsleeve and the material rides up, revealing the strange tattoos that undulate and curl on their own like they are coming alive on his skin, staring up at them both like malignant eyes. The air grows dark and stifling, and the mist begins again, rising expectantly around the two teenagers.

The brunette stumbles back, eyes staring out of her lovely head, uncertain of what she has just seen.

"No!" the boy shouts, and his voice carries across the room. The rest of the cafeteria falls silent, heads turning. The boy yanks his sleeves back down, so hard the fabric nearly tears from the strength of his misery. And yet the fog doesn't lift. It rolls over and around him so that, to his cousin's eyes, the denseness of the shadow obscures him, the form behind him rising once more to mimic the shape of that brooding mask, that lady in black.

Neither the teaching assistant nor the rest of the students see this woman. Not even the tattooed boy seems to realize her closeness. His face is washed of all color, and he is clinging to the table before him, hunched over in pain.

Several things happen.

Flocks of birds crash through the window.

They are missing their heads.

They hit the walls hard: *thud, thud, thud*. They crash into plates and trays, into water fountains and people. Several smash into the lighting fixtures overhead before dropping down, suddenly motionless, and nearly missing a group of girls huddled in a corner.

The students begin to scream. The boy's cousin claps a hand over her mouth, stunned by what she has just witnessed.

Without another word, the tattooed boy takes off—past the cafeteria doors and down the corridors, bursting out of the school's main doors and barreling down the street, with the woman's shadow fluttering after him.

"Tarquin!" His cousin follows him. She is quick enough to catch sight of him, with the strange darkness surrounding his head like a crown, before he disappears around the corner. "I'm going after him!" she calls out to other teachers who poke their heads out of their rooms, curious. She gestures back inside, where the screaming continues to drift out, where the dead birds still litter the floor.

"Take care of them, Jen!" she tells her friend who has come running up, eyes wide.

"What are you going to do?"

The young woman does not answer her. Already, she is running.

But boys are light of feet and quick of temper, and he is soon lost in the busy afternoon of cars and people. The teacher's assistant pauses, looking this way and that, hoping to catch a glimpse of him. But the crowd flows past her, unyielding and unrepentant.

It is then that she sees the woman in white.

I am standing at the corner of a busy intersection, my face hidden under a ruined cobweb of hair. The girl sees me like a man might see an oasis in a dried desert—disbelieving, certain that her senses play with her mind, convinced this is nothing more than a mistake, a puzzle of flesh.

I lift my hand and point at something in the far distance. The young woman takes a step forward, her own arm extending, reaching for this strange creature. She is convinced that she will be reassured if she touches this apparition and feels the sensation of skin and bones underneath her own. But in the space between moments I move, and she finds herself standing alone, with only people swarming past.

She turns in the direction I pointed and, because she can think of no other alternative, follows this road.

She stops again along a boulevard, her path lost. A pedestrian light turns green across the street. Once again she catches sight of the woman in white gliding through the rush of people, and I do little to blend in. I lift my head momentarily and the teaching assistant glimpses black hair streaming down past sightless eyes, before I am once more gone in the maze of briefcases and shopping bags.

The young woman makes her decision. She takes off after me, following the bread crumbs I am strewing in her path. Her pace quickens as her certainty grows, and she pauses only to call out apologies and excuses as she jostles against other men and women scurrying past.

She finally catches sight of the tattooed boy. He sits inside a white car. His eyes are half closed, and his head lolls against the seat. But the man closing the door beside him is not his father. It is a blond man with bright eyes and youthful features, and he is smiling.

"Wait!" The girl is frantic. Heads turn in her direction as she fights against the flow of people walking past: an old man in a wheelchair, a dog walker with three German shepherds, two baby carriages. "Wait! Stop him! Tarquin!"

But the man starts the car and drives away, leaving her helpless by the curb. Inside the car, the teenager turns his head, puzzled.

"Did someone call me?" he asks, his voice slurred.

"I didn't hear anyone," the Smiling Man says gently. "Go back to sleep."

The car speeds on. The young woman watches it leave before she looks around and does the next best thing.

"Taxi!"

"For the last time, Jen—this is *not* a joke." She speaks into her phone with a mixture of annoyance and agitation, as the taxi speeds down the street in pursuit of the white car. "I think Tarquin Halloway has been kidnapped by a man in a white Ford, and I want you to call the police. No, I don't have their number just lying around. Yes, 911's been busy for the last five minutes, and I'm not entirely sure why. That's why I want *you* to call instead while I... Yes, I'll let you know as soon as I figure out where they're heading. No, I don't know what the hell happened with those birds. Yes, I'll be back as soon as I find Tark."

"Is this for real, lady?" The taxi driver looks alarmed. "We're after some pervert on the run?"

"I don't know yet." The young woman's eyes are glued to the white car just ahead, which is turning onto a smaller, quieter street at the outskirts of town. They lose it for a few minutes after it speeds up and turns a sharp corner, and it takes some more searching before she finally catches a glimpse of the car as it turns into a small driveway, almost hidden by a tall grove of trees. She gestures at the driver to stop at the opposite side of the street.

"I'll be getting off here. Keep the change."

"You sure you don't want me to stick around, miss?"

She pauses. "Can you use your radio to call the police?"

"Yeah, I think so. I mean, I can radio my boss and he can—"

"Do that." She hands him a couple of bills and gets out of the car.

"I think you ought to wait for the cops to get here, miss. If there's some wacko on the loose, I don't think you ought to be looking for him alone…"

"I don't think I can wait that long. Just call the police as quickly as you can." She runs toward the row of houses, while the taxi driver picks up his radio and speaks hurriedly into it. But by the time he gets out of the car, intent on following the teaching assistant, he stops. She is nowhere to be seen.

She is not afraid, not at first. She is careful not to attract too much attention, though her nerves are frayed and adrenaline shoots through her network of veins. The house is nestled on a tiny cul-de-sac, one of only three houses there. It stands against a back-drop of afternoon sky, the sun bleeding through the clouds. A still calm descends as she nears the parked white car. The hood is warm when she touches it, but its occupants are missing.

The cab driver's right, the teacher's assistant thinks. *There are a million reasons why I shouldn't be here alone. I've watched enough slasher movies to know this.*

But she knows that as the minutes tick by, her cousin draws ever closer to danger. Her last conversation with his father drifts into her mind, and she is ashamed that she is unable to keep her promise of watching over him. It is a part of her nature to be protective, and this flaw sometimes overrules her caution.

She tries the door and is not surprised to find it locked. She wrestles against the idea that she could be arrested for breaking and entering, tries to imagine herself serving time in jail stripes, and decides to chance it. She circles the house and finds a small window opened partway—enough for her to be able to squirm inside.

There is no one inside the first room she enters, which is a kitchen. Knives of varying sizes line the wall, gleaming in the dull light. Grocery bags take up one side of the kitchen island, filled with vegetables and canned goods. Everything appears to be in its place, tidy. There is nothing out of the ordinary here. She waits at first; frightened, certain she's been found out—but the minutes go by, and no one comes. The house is quiet; not a creature stirs.

For a moment she feels foolish, embarrassed. Could she be mistaken, after all? She takes out her phone to call her friend and is annoyed by the lack of mobile signal in the area.

She turns just in time to catch a glimpse of me drifting into the next room, head bowed, feet barely touching the ceiling.

She is taken aback and wonders briefly if she is going crazy on top of everything else, but she realizes she has come too far now to turn back. She grabs a small knife as a precaution, then follows me into the next room and sees me standing before a large wooden door. She blinks, and I disappear.

By all outward appearances, it could have been a closet or a storage space, or even a small bedroom, the type allotted for guests. But when the teaching assistant pulls the door open, all she sees is a set of stairs, leading down into night.

It is all she can do to take that first step down. It creaks slightly under her weight, not loud enough to echo into the narrow space, but enough that she becomes more aware of the darkness. Her descent is slow and careful, and for the first time, she wishes she had looked around for a flashlight to bring. But before she changes her mind, she reaches the bottom.

There is a bulb hanging at the end of the stairs and another door before her. The young woman swallows hard, silently counts to ten, and pushes it open.

Inside, the tattooed boy is nestled against a small cot on one side of the room, fast asleep and unharmed in every way that she can see, much to her relief. A small candle has been lit beside him.

Large pipes run parallel across one wall, gurgling water and sewage. The room itself carries a dank smell of rotten wood and moss.

The young woman looks around for other signs of life. Finding none, she hurries to him, feels his forehead, and sighs with relief upon noting his steady pulse, his measured breathing. "Tark? Tark, wake up."

But the boy only murmurs something unintelligible and sinks back into slumber.

She takes one step, two steps toward him, then gets no farther. Something crashes painfully against the side of her head, and the last thing she sees before blacking out is me, standing over her crumpled form, head twisted enough to one side that a disfigured eye stares back down at her, black against a pale, stark face.

CHAPTER EIGHT

THE SMILING MAN

"Wakey, wakey, sleeping beauty."

This is the first thing the teacher's assistant hears as she struggles back to consciousness. A light shines from somewhere above and distorts her vision. She shakes her head, attempting to dispel this hurt, and finds that she cannot move. Someone has lashed a series of ropes around her legs and arms, imprisoning her against a hard bed. She can do nothing more than move her head a few degrees in either direction.

A man moves into her line of vision. He is the same one she saw driving the white car with the drowsing teenager in his passenger seat.

"Welcome back to the land of the living," the Smiling Man says. "Though I am sorry to say you won't be staying here very long."

The girl tries to sit up, struggling in terror against her bonds, but the Smiling Man has done this many times before, and they hold fast. She opens her mouth to scream, but the man merely laughs as her cries bounce off the walls. "Nobody's going to hear you this far down, sweetheart. I made sure of it." He grins in a disarming way, but his eyes remain blank and hooded, unable to absorb so much as a glimmer of light.

"I called the police," the girl gasps out, unwilling to surrender. "They'll be here soon, and they'll catch you."

The Smiling Man

take him, take him now

shrugs this off, like it is of little importance to him.

"It's quite a drive from the nearest police station, especially with the rush hour. There aren't many police in this town anymore, not after the recession. And besides"—he leans in close so she could smell his light, delicate perfume, the strong decay of eggs in his breath—"by the time they get here I will be gone," he whispers. "And you will still be dead."

He moves toward the boy and strokes his head fondly. "You're a little too old for me," he tells the teaching assistant. "Too old. I like them young. The younger, the prettier, the better. This one's older than I'm used to, but he's got such a pretty face." His fingers find a trail down the side of the boy's jawline.

"But what to do with you?" He throws the covers off one table, revealing an assortment of knives, of strange and twisted surgical instruments. The girl's struggles increase in earnest, and she screams again. "Never had anyone as old as you before. Not my type. Doesn't mean we can't have some fun, though, right?" He selects one of the larger knives and advances toward the now-terrified young woman, still smiling as kindly as a choirboy.

"I think I'll start with you first. I like to take my time when it comes to my toys, and I won't have that as long as I'm in the house, thanks to you. By the time they arrive and find your body, I'll be far away with my little boy, and no one will ever find us."

Something rustles at the corner of his eye, and a faint gurgling reaches his ears. The Smiling Man

crushhimscreamcrushhim

turns his head, frowning at the distraction. But the boy continues to slumber atop the bed, and there is no one else present. Satisfied, he turns back.

He seizes the young woman's wrist, ignoring how she cries out, how she tries to push him away. "Maybe I should take a little bit of you as a souvenir," he says, thoughtfully. "A keepsake for the short time we had together, if you'd like. So a part of you will always be with my—Tarquin, didn't you say his name was?—my Tarquin here. It's the least I can do for you."

The tattooed boy is still sleeping on the cot, unmoving. His feet are shackled, and his face is worn. Neither the girl nor the Smiling Man

crushkillcrushkillKILLKILL

sees the small blanket of black that rises around his form, though in the small trickle of light it seems larger somehow, like it gains its strength from places such as these.

The knife blade sinks into the young woman's finger. Her screams grow louder.

Just as suddenly, the light above their heads breaks off, shattering. Over the sound of the young woman's wailing, the Smiling Man is cursing. He fumbles for a lighter that he has set down on the table, a small spark of flame igniting as the burning flint meets a candle. He holds this aloft, raising it up over his head to survey the bulb on the ceiling. He finds nothing wrong with it, except that it will no longer work.

He lowers the candle. He sees the faint outline of the boy on the bed and is satisfied. He starts to turn back toward the young woman, who is still struggling to free herself from her restraints.

Something else blocks his vision.

The Smiling Man finds himself looking at a

woman

on the ceiling. The glow of candlelight catches only her face, her long hair hanging down, and her bright black eyes. She is only inches away, and she

gurgles.

It is the Smiling Man's turn to scream, and the brief light is suddenly extinguished.

The young woman freezes as noises begin to erupt all around her, the sounds of frantic combat. She can hear the Smiling Man yelling at something to get away, threatening the unseen with death and worse. A table is overturned, and she hears the sound of several metallic objects hitting the floor, scattering. Blows rain down against one wall.

And then there is silence again. The young woman strains to hear more, fearful of the outcome.

Something moves along the floor; more muttered cursing. Another light flickers on, revealing the Smiling Man holding a flashlight he has found inside one of the shelves. His clothes look ripped in several places, and thin, bloody trails mark his chest and upper arms, which he has scraped against his own knives and surgical equipment. He is no longer smiling. He is still sprawled on the floor beside the cot, panting and, for the first time since the young woman entered the tiny basement, afraid and no longer in control.

"What the hell was that?" he snarls. His face is twisting, the mask coming away so that the murderer underneath that gentle, genial facade is finally looking out. "Where are you, you bitch? I'm gonna kill you!" He swings the flashlight around the room, but other than the young woman, still trapped and whimpering, and the motionless tattooed boy, everything is silent. He swings the light up toward the ceiling, but there is no longer anyone there.

There is a cracking sound behind him, and something touches his foot. He looks back.

I am underneath the boy's cot, watching him with wide, unblinking

eyes.

Shouting, the Smiling Man lunges forward, kicking desperately with his legs, but he continues to be pulled inexorably back despite his best efforts. He lands hard on his stomach and tries to crawl away, but his fingernails only carve deep grooves into the floor, leaving long scratches as he fights, shrill and squealing, and as he is yanked in quick, sporadic jerks underneath the bed, where I

kill him

am waiting

for

   him.

The light goes out a second time.

The young woman does not know how long she lies in the darkness, waiting. The Smiling Man has stopped screaming, and silence now takes his place. All she can hear is the house settling around her and the absence of anything else alive in the room.

Her finger stings. She can feel the blood trickling down her hand from the wound. Yet she grits her teeth, muffling her cries as best she can, as she tugs again at the ropes binding her.

The overhead bulb flickers back to life, light filling the room for the third time, and the young woman starts, blinking her eyes at the unexpected glare.

The tattooed boy has risen from the cot. His eyes are open, and he is crouching with his back toward his cousin, looking under the bed where the remains of the Smiling Man have been wedged into the small space, so small that it is not likely the body would have fit by natural methods. The dead man's mouth is still open, like he has not yet finished screaming, but his face is bloodless and bloated and grotesque. The tattooed boy does not react to the sight, but the young woman squeezes her eyes shut, not wanting to look at the corpse any further.

When she opens her eyes again, the boy is standing over her.

"Tarquin," she whispers, relieved that he is unharmed. "Tark, you have to help me. Cut me loose from these ropes. We need to call the police as soon as we can…"

The boy does not say anything. He continues to look down at her, and only then does the girl realize that there is a strangeness in his manner that has not been there in the past. He has a peculiar smile on his face, but an expression of aberrant emptiness. There is no expression in his eyes, and he gives no indication he recognizes her.

"Tark?..."

The boy's attention is riveted on her wound, the red dripping down her mangled finger. He moves farther up the gurney. His sleeves are rolled up almost to his shoulders.

Now the young woman sees the boy's tattoos up close. Several more lines of obscure writing ride up the length of his arm, beginning at the strange seals that mark each of his wrists.

There is blood on one of the seals, at the back of his right hand. As she watches, this blood disappears quickly into his skin as the seal pulses like it is alive. The ink fades in and out of view, matching the cadence and the rhythm of the shadow that continues to surround him, wrapping around in the air like it is a living, breathing creature all on its own.

The boy takes his cousin's wounded hand. His touch is dry and clammy, as cold as death. He turns her palm down, and they both watch as the blood oozes out of her fingers and splatters against the seal on his left wrist.

This blood also is soon absorbed into the boy's flesh, the seal lapping up all traces of it. The seal now throbs and ripples across his skin, just like its counterpart on his other arm.

The shadow behind the boy further expands, and the teacher's assistant finally sees the face that emerges from within its confines. It is another woman, this time one garbed in black. The strangeness of her face is caused by a round porcelain mask—eerily similar to the faces of the dolls in the room sheltering the boy's mother—that hides most of her features. But parts of it have crumbled away. Ruined skin and a drooping eye stare out from behind the mask, repulsive and hideous.

The young woman screams again, but the boy does not see the woman. He moves and jerks about like a puppet. Both seals continue to crawl and twist like live snakes underneath the boy's flesh. The woman in black reaches out for the teacher's assistant, horrible triumph etched in her ruined eye.

But she rears back when she sees

me

standing behind the teaching assistant, who cries out as she, too, spots me.

I meet the masked woman's livid gaze—for what feels like a few seconds, for what feels like a millennium—before the shadow takes a step back, and her face is soon swallowed up by the fog that hovers around the boy for several more seconds and then disappears abruptly with little warning. When she is gone, the boy collapses.

"Who are you?" The young woman whimpers, but that is not a question I can easily answer. I look down at her again, and I see her jerk in surprise.

For I no longer stand before her as a

ruined

horror; now she sees me as a girl; young, my hair coiled up around my head like I often wore it, with brown eyes and skin a pale white from the absence of sun rather than a mark of the long dead. I look at her looking back at the girl I once was, and the ghosts of the little dead children, freed from the Smiling Man's taint, gather around me glowing.

The young woman faints.

She recalls very little of what happens in the interim, only rousing herself when she hears shouts and cries from outside the room. She holds her breath at first, fearful, and knows no greater relief than when the voices become more distinct, drumming down the stairs.

"Tarquin Halloway! Callie Starr! This is the police! Can you hear us? Call out to us if you can!"

"I'm here!" the young woman screams, voice hoarse. "I'm here! Help us! Please, help us!"

For a moment, she is afraid that her pleas will go unheard, but after several more minutes, the door to the basement opens, and beams of light stream into the room.

"Miss Callie Starr? Stay calm, miss, we're going to help you. Are you hurt anywhere?"

"My hand..." the teacher's assistant whispers. "And Tarquin..."

"Don't worry about it, ma'am. The medics are here. We're going to get you out as soon as we can."

"He's okay." Another of the men reports, checking the fallen teenager. "Pulse is normal, no signs of injury on him."

The young woman feels like laughing, and she does, startling her rescuers. No signs of injury on Tarquin! And yet the tattoos on his arms! The seals thriving like little creatures, feasting on his skin!

"Oh my God," she hears another of the men say. They shine their light on the other bed, revealing the Smiling Man, except his head is now missing. Shuddering, she turns away.

Just before her strength fails again, she imagines she can see me as before, the woman in white with long hair and an ashen face, now standing in a darker corner of the room. I am surrounded by strange little lights, bobbing up and down as if they sit on an unseen river that flows around my frame. One by one, they move against the air, like shooting stars that rise up instead of falling down. I say nothing, only watching as they float into the refuge of darkness.

Callie Starr closes her eyes and does not open them again for some time.

CHAPTER NINE

DOLLS

The teacher's assistant has never been here before, although it is every bit as frightening as she had imagined it to be. People in loose robes (sixteen) stare coldly at her as she walks past, suspicious of how she is free to leave this place whenever she wishes to, when they cannot. Some people ignore her completely, bursting into shrill, hysterical laughter at voices no one else can hear (twelve). Others prefer the company of their closets or their potted plants, conducting animated conversations with the imaginary things that live within (ten).

People call this place the Remney Psychiatric Institute.

The teacher's assistant looks tired. The bruises marring her face are lighter than two weeks ago, enough that they are easily hidden under a thin layer of makeup. The little finger on her right hand remains heavily bandaged, and she moves her arm with stiffness that suggests a midpoint between hurting and recovery. While sensitive to the touch, the small wound on the side of her head no longer requires dressing. She is pale, and the bright fluorescent lights overhead do nothing to hide her pain.

She has been released from the hospital with her doctor's permission, avoiding the well-wishes and well-intentioned worry of visitors and friends as she did. But she cannot rest, not just yet. There is something else she must do first.

The White Shirt is nervous, and understandably so. He has agreed with extreme reluctance to allow the young assistant visiting rights, despite Remney's stern rules restricting this to immediate family members only. But because the tattooed boy's father personally requests this, the White Shirt unlocks the door leading into the Japanese woman's room and steps back to allow the young woman entry.

The shoji screens are gone, but the dolls are still in their wooden stands, and like many others before her, this sight makes the young woman very uncomfortable. The Japanese woman sits on a chair at the center of the room, staring at nothing. She makes no sound, gives no signal that she is aware of the young woman's presence. Nervous, the young woman hovers uncertainly a few feet away, torn between advancing and retreating.

"Mrs. Halloway? Aunt Yoko?"

The woman rocks back and forth, eyes glued to the wall before her, staring at the large carpeted stand filled with imperial dolls.

The teacher's assistant tries again. "Aunt Yoko? My name is Calliope Starr. I'm Doug Halloway's niece. Tarquin's cousin."

A faint ghost of a smile curves along the older woman's mouth. "Tarquin?"

"Yes," the young woman says, encouraged. "Your son, Tarquin?"

"He's a very lovely boy," the woman says. "He was a beautiful baby. So sweet. So very innocent. That's what's wrong with him, you know. If there had been more cruelty in his nature, like normal boys have, he would not be suffering as he does now. Still—such a beautiful baby boy. Has something happened to him?" Alarm flickers in the woman's eyes, and she attempts to stand. The White Shirt guarding the door stiffens, prepared to summon for assistance if necessary. "Has something happened to my Tarquin?"

"Nothing's happened to him," the teacher's assistant says hurriedly. "Tarquin's all right. He's safe."

"Liar!" The woman shakes her head. "Tarquin isn't safe. And it's all my fault. My fault, my fault..."

"Aunt Yoko, it isn't your fault—"

"It's all my fault! I had no choice!" The woman sinks back into her chair, but her rocking motions grow more frantic and agitated. "He had to be sacrificed! I had no choice! She would have killed more!"

"Aunt Yoko!" The teaching assistant takes hold of the woman's shoulders, steadying her. Pain travels up her injured shoulder, but she does not let go until the woman ceases her violent thrashing, her voice now reduced to soft whimpers. The White Shirt relaxes, though still alert. "Aunt Yoko, who would have killed more?"

"I had to," the woman whispers. "I had to stop her."

"Who? The woman in black?"

A shudder racks the woman's body, and she moans.

"I think that's enough, Miss Starr," the White Shirt says disapprovingly.

"No! No. She has to know. Do you have a mother, my dear?"

"Yes. Linda Starr, Uncle Doug's sister."

"I see it now. There is something of Douglas in your eyes. Tarquin was always too young to remember the mother I once was with him—the mother I should have been. How is it that you can see her? Why do you see the woman with the mask?"

"I...I don't know."

"I looked up to her, you know. She was the best of us all. Chiyo had always been perfect, could do no wrong. But even she could not prevent such hate from taking hold of her. I tried, but the sealing was incomplete. The ritual had not been performed in such a long time, and none of us knew how well it would work, if it even would. But we had to try. Poor, poor Chiyo. And my Tarquin..." Her face crumples, and she ducks her head, long hair streaming down her face.

"Did you send *her* as well?" she asks, head still lowered. "The white ghost?"

"The white ghost?" the teacher's assistant repeats, taken aback.

"The *yuurei*—a spirit that cannot rest. The lady in white. The lady with the broken neck. The woman who cannot rest. Did you send her to help my son?"

"I...I don't..."

"I saw her," the frail woman insists. "I saw her on the ceiling, hanging down. I thought she meant to harm my husband and my son, but now I know she is here for a much different purpose. The binding seals on my son attract her, as they do all *yuurei*. But the woman in black repels even her. Even now I see the woman in white, standing behind you."

The young woman swallows hard and, trembling, turns—but sees nothing.

"Seals?" she asks. "The tattoos on your son's body…they're binding seals?"

"Five seals, arranged in a star pattern. Here, and here…" The woman touches her chest, then the backs of her hands. Finally, her fingers drift down her sides to rest on the rise of her hips. "And here. But the ritual has only partly succeeded. Little by little, the masked woman is breaking free of the chains that bind her to my Tarquin. I know she has broken many of those seals. She knows she is close."

The woman grips the teaching assistant's arm. "Promise me you will protect my son. Promise me you will tell my husband that he must return to where it all began, to lift the curse. He will not believe you. He will not understand. But you must convince him."

"Return to where?"

But something else distracts the woman. She rises from her chair, stepping toward the platform, and lifts an empress doll off its stand. Taking a tiny pearl comb from her dresser, she returns to her seat with the doll settled on her lap. Now she combs its hair, a doting mother.

"Have you ever been to the *Hina-matsuri*?" Her voice is calm once more, placid. "It is a time-honored festival, celebrated throughout

Japan. My father was a celebrated dollmaker, and my sister and I grew up surrounded by his creations. People would buy his dolls and bring them out for luck during the *Hina-matsuri*. But dolls are useful in other ways, as well. One can, for instance, use dolls as a sacrifice—a way to capture evil spirits and keep them trapped within their bodies for as long as it takes to exorcise their malice. Did you know what dolls like these are called in Japan? *Ningyo.* 'One of human shape.'"

She pauses, staring off into the distance, while her hand continues to stroke the empress's hair.

"But there also exist spirits so powerful that mere dolls cannot contain them. For this, another type of sacrifice must be used—a living human being, an innocent.

"For many long years, Chiyo had endured as such a sacrifice. But then the spirits took over, transforming her into the revenant she is now. To overcome her ghost, I was forced to create a new sacrifice…

"Was it wrong for a mother to sacrifice her son to protect the lives of others around me, those who looked to me for protection? I do not know. I was so sure of myself back then, so sure I could cleanse him from her taint eventually. But I could not."

She smiles then, sadly. "Tarquin must have told you how I have tried to kill him many times. I thought it was the only choice I had left. But there is one more thing I can do for him. After tonight, my son will no longer suffer from my mistakes. This will end, one way or another." She places the empress on her bed, rises to select another doll, and begins the same painstaking process all over again. "But if I fail, he must return."

"Return to where?" The teacher's assistant could easily dismiss the woman's words as nothing more than ramblings. Even the White Shirt lounging by the door is no longer listening, now that the threat of violence has passed.

But the young teacher has seen the woman in black. She has seen the woman in white and is now aware of how strange things may lurk, unseen to the eye. She has seen the Smiling Man's corpse. She has seen her cousin's face, as blank and as paper-white as all the dolls in this room, and her own blood curdling against the seals on his skin.

The woman looks back at her, and for the first time, there is clarity in her gaze. "Yagen Valley," she says. "They must return to the little dolls of Yagen Valley, to my sisters. To the fear, where it all began."

The young woman leaves several minutes later with more questions, rather than the answers she seeks. The woman is alone. She selects another doll, running the small comb through its glossy black hair. Once this is completed to her satisfaction, she lifts the doll to the light, gazing into its face. She must like what she sees, for she sets the doll down—not in its usual place on the stands, but on the floor next to her chair.

She takes another doll and does the same thing, placing it down on the ground once she is done and reaching for yet another— until finally, eight dolls surround her in a circle, all facing inward. Their blank faces bore into the woman's, awaiting her next move.

It is foolish, this thing that she attempts.

"It may be so," she says to me, as I stand in the corner of the darkened room and watch her, "but it must be done."

There is a knock at the door. One of the White Shirts arrives with dinner and her medication. In exchange, the woman hands him a small letter and asks him to post it on her behalf as quickly as possible. When he leaves, she carefully spits the tablets back into her hand and hides them in a tiny space between the wall and the dresser where several other pills gather dust.

From behind several dolls, she extracts four slim candles and a box of matches, taken when the White Shirts were distracted elsewhere. She lights one of the candles and tilts it to allow the tallow to drip onto the floor. She moves slowly, and when the flames flicker briefly against her fingers she gives no cry of pain, making little sound at all. She does not stop until a perfect circle of dried wax surrounds all eight dolls.

She now lights the other candles in turn, setting them down in all four directions outside the circle. Lastly, she steps inside the ring with the empress doll, seating herself at its center. She closes her eyes and begins to chant softly, once again in that obscure, melodic language.

Nothing happens. Not at first.

There are no windows in the room, yet a breeze picks up. A noiseless wind begins to whip at the hair of the dolls on their shelves, wrapping around their faces and blindfolding their eyes with their own dark locks. The wooden stands splinter, seemingly on their own. The bed behind the woman, though bolted down, lifts up once, then crashes back down against the floor.

This does not frighten the woman, who continues her chanting. Something takes umbrage at her impertinence. The shaking grows louder, more agitated. Dolls rain down as shelves dislodge themselves from the screws in the walls. The room itself seems gripped in the throes of an earthquake that grows fiercer with every minute that passes. Claw marks appear against grooves in the ceiling, long deep scratches raking down.

And still the woman chants. The eight dolls remain upright despite this terrible haunting, and the candles sputter and wink out briefly, but just as quickly resume their light.

The black fog appears just outside of the wax circle. Unlike during her previous appearances, the woman in black seems tangible, solid. Her face emerges from the writhing darkness, a ruin of skin and clot. More of the mask she wears has fallen, and now two staring sockets look out from a hideously disfigured face, flecked and mottled.

The woman called Yoko lifts the empress. The doll stares serenely back at the black abomination with its blank, colorless eyes.

"Begone!" the Japanese woman cries, and for the first time she is alive, more animated than I have ever seen her. "Leave us alone!" More sutras flow from her lips.

The woman in black hovers in the air, motionless. Then she lifts a hand as if to ward off an invisible blow, but against her will, she is slowly pulled toward the empress doll. The other woman does not budge. She is unmoving, triumphant.

The woman in black lifts her head again, and all the hate is in her eyes. Then the wind dies. The candle's flame flickers out briefly, and when it returns, only the Japanese woman and I remain inside the room. The woman in black is gone.

The Japanese woman waits for a few moments, panting heavily. When all is finally quiet, she lowers the doll and looks at its upturned face. Its eyes are now a solid, unending black.

The woman begins to laugh—silently, then hysterically—relieved it is now over. With the empress doll still in hand, she takes a step outside of the wax circle, moving back toward the doll's stand.

Behind her, one of the dolls in the circle slowly leans over and topples forward to land face-first on the floor.

The woman turns, shocked. As she watches, the other seven dolls follow, sinking to land on their faces, one after the other in the same manner as the first.

She looks down at the empress doll in her hand.

A mask stares back at her, and behind it that maimed, hideous face.

The woman says a curious thing.

"*Oneesan*," she whimpers, beseeching, as ragged nails claw their way up her arms and shoulders, the woman in black extending to her full height. The empress doll falls at the Japanese woman's feet, its head torn off.

The woman screams, but by then it is already too late.

When it is done, the woman in black stares at me. From behind her mask, she smiles.

The night passes quietly enough for the other inmates at

Remney's, but when one of the White Shirts comes to check on the woman, that peace is soon shattered. She bursts out of the room in such hysterics that it becomes difficult to distinguish her from her patients.

Someone has cut off the heads of all one hundred and eight dolls, their faces charred by some unknown fire. The room is in disarray with the bed and chair overturned, and faint scorch marks encompass one side of the wall. The headless dolls are lined up in small rows beside the broken bed, which is now drenched in blood.

And underneath this bed they find the one hundred and ninth head.

CHAPTER TEN

UNDERSTANDING

The air smells like a hundred years of memories. The teacher's assistant reads through articles scrolling on a large computer screen. Piles of dusty newspapers lie strewn on the floor. There are few people in the local library today and fewer still in this small, musty section of the building that many have already forgotten. Old things still flourish here.

The young woman sits hunched over a large table and scrolls through countless sheets of yellowed, preserved paper. In this small room, she logs on to the Internet and spends several minutes assuring her mother that all is right with the world, lying about her lack of injuries and the exaggeration of the media. Then she begins her research and, within an hour, finds a series of reported murders strangely similar to the one she has just lived through:

Mutilated Body found in Houston, Texas
Bloated Body Located in Florida Swamps
Unidentified Body in Mexico
Remains Found in Brazil

Gruesome Discovery in Queensland, Australia

Body Found Floating in River, Philippines

The list goes on, and the young woman finds the details disturbing. Bodies discovered in the same way: faces bloated and distended as if held underwater indefinitely; the fear in their faces; their eyes rolled back until only the whites show. Of the fifty-eight articles she has found, only twenty-three of the victims have ever been identified. Most were drifters, meeting their deaths in lands far from the countries of their birth. Of the twenty-three identified, thirteen had been arrested on previous charges, many of them sexual offenses. Most have been suspects in other missing persons cases, all of which involved children and teenagers. Five have been posthumously convicted for these crimes.

The young teacher leans back against her chair, thinking.

She tries to look up everything known about Blake Mosses, but has little to show for her efforts. Except for the numerous articles written about his death, no other matches turn up for the dead man at the Holly Oaks apartment. The only telling clue was the police's recent discovery of a hair fiber wedged within his floorboards, and the results will not be determined for many more months.

She types in a different name next: Quintilian Saetern.

Throughout news reports of the Smiling Man's murder, she lay in seclusion, unfettered by the cameras and news reporters attempting to reach her hospital bed for an interview, only to be repulsed by nurses and policemen. The Smiling Man was less taciturn about hiding his name than Blake Mosses had been, and by the time she had healed enough to leave, the reporters had lost interest in her, having discovered the Smiling Man's past through other more conventional means.

She discovers that Quintilian Saetern's real name was Quintilian Densmore, formerly of Massachusetts. A string of juvenile offenses followed him into adulthood, and at twenty years of age he was charged with the attempted rape of a ten-year-old girl and served five years. Two months after his release from jail, he inherited a substantial fortune from his father and began traveling extensively. The reported disappearances of more young women and children over the years bore the marks of his killing spree. His first conviction had taught him one thing: dead people tell no tales.

The police have no suspects in his killing. They have interviewed the teacher's assistant and the tattooed boy, hoping to find more leads, but have so far met with little success. The boy has no recollection of his time in the basement, and the young woman tells them nothing about me or the masked woman.

Though with no further clues, the detectives are of the same opinion as most of the residents in Applegate—that the guilty party deserved neither an arrest nor a prison sentence, but a medal and a commendation from the governor himself, for killing Quintilian Densmore. Still, two murders in so short a time have caused an uneasy ripple in Applegate. Uncertainty has gripped the town, and people no longer feel as safe as they once did.

It is an unfortunate side effect of my work, but one worth the consequences.

Here in this moldy section of the public library, the girl starts again with the basics of what she already knows. For one, two, three, four hours, she scrolls through the microfilm. I lean over her shoulder to read what she has found.

1970—*Mutilated Body Found in Houston, Texas.* Suspected murderer Gavin Hollencamp found dead at his apartment on September 14. Water found in his lungs, along with his heavily corroded face, suggested death by drowning. Advanced decomposition of his skin indicated at least five days spent underwater, though many witnesses claimed to have seen Hollencamp alive the day before his death. Revenge believed to be the motive for the killing, but as all known suspects have solid alibis, police are left with no leads. Suspected of murdering ten-year-old Lisa Brooks two years before, though eventually acquitted due to a court technicality. Still an open case.

1995—*Bloated Body Located in Florida Swamps.* Body identified as a Mathelson Smith from Boise, Idaho. Lower half of corpse believed to have been eaten by alligators. Smith was wanted for questioning in connection with the disappearance of Lydia Small, aged ten, two months earlier after she was last seen in his company. Characteristics of the water found in his lungs suggested groundwater such as that found in artesian wells, indicating that the man had not drowned in the swamps as originally thought. Police suspect possible foul play but possess few leads.

2004—*Gruesome Discovery in Queensland, Australia.* Fully clothed body found washed up on the beach in North Narrabeen,

Sydney, and soon identified as a Patrick Neville, fifty-two, local car salesman. According to witnesses, Neville was on a yacht with business associates when he "looked down into the water and gave this bone-chilling scream shortly before falling overboard." Others claim Neville was yanked into the water—but they could provide no description of what pulled him in. Sharks and other large fish are not known to inhabit this particular coast. The medical examiner could not explain the several days' worth of decay on the deceased's face, despite the accident taking place only hours earlier. Two years before his death, Neville was one of five suspects questioned regarding the disappearances of several children in the northern Sydney area. Police have no leads.

The young woman feels hair brushing against the side of her head and sees from the corner of her eyes tendrils of black, stringy hair and a white face inches beside hers. She whirls around, clutching at the table with her hands for support, but the apparition is gone.

"You're here, aren't you?" she asks the darkness, still breathing hard.

Her eyes fall on several small piles of newspapers and binders, dusty from disuse. Her eyes widen for a moment before her face settles into a bright, almost calculating, expression. She rises from her chair and begins to lug stacks of these newspapers over by her chair. I count them.

One stack, two stacks.

Finished, she returns to her chair, though there is now an air of urgency and nervous excitement about her.

Five stacks, six stacks.

She takes a deep breath and then holds it. Her hands are clenched, and she is biting her lip.

Eight stacks. Nine stacks.

She waits.

Nothing happens. Relief and disappointment fills her, and her hands lower.

And just as suddenly, the ninth stack of newspapers begin to fold in on itself in front of her horrified eyes. Inch after inch it is crushed by unseen, powerful hands, until it is now a third of its previous size, the paper so heavily compacted that removing an individual sheaf becomes impossible.

No

nines.

There is silence in the room, except for the sounds of the young teacher's quiet, panicked breathing, fearful of retribution for her insolence.

And then just outside in the hallway, something lands with a heavy thump.

The young woman jumps, another scream leaving her mouth before she is able to stop herself. But the minutes tick by and nothing untoward happens and so, with shaking feet, she ventures to where the sound came from, out into the long hallway leading back into the library.

There is no one else around. One of the books had fallen from the shelves, landing facedown on the floor.

The girl picks it up, turning it over to see the page it was open to.

The large volume is titled *Popular Japanese Destinations*, and the open page shows a picturesque view of a large, rocky wasteland dotted by majestic peaks and yellow hot springs.

"If you're an adventurous traveler with a taste for the strange and the macabre," the caption begins, "Mount Osore (fondly known as *Osorezan* by the locals) on Aomori, Mutsu province, may be right up your alley. Known for its Bodai Temple and peaceful, if rather desolate surroundings. A small road leads into the mostly uninhabited Yagen Valley, where visitors can enjoy an unusual mixture of uncivilized nature and uncrowded hot springs."

The young woman looks around. She does not see me but speaks anyway.

"Thank you," Callie whispers.

The tattooed boy is hiding.

It is night, and the lights have gone out in other houses. The only sources of illumination are the strange moon looking down at him from the window and the faint artificial glow of the lampposts on the streets below.

Something is in the room with him. This much he knows, and that is why he hides. Shadows steal across the ceiling; boards creak and groan as the house settles down for the night; and he is hiding.

It starts with the mirror, where he can see a small reflection of himself beside his bed, huddled in the corner of the room and whispering "oh crap oh crap oh crap oh crap" in quiet staccato.

From inside this mirror, a long, spindly hand reaches out, and something forbidding and black forces its way through the surface and climbs out. The boy's breathing grows ragged, his heart racing.

Just as suddenly, the lampposts outside die out one by one in rapid succession. Only one directly across the street from the house remains, sputtering in and out, casting darkness one moment and then fleeting, rudimentary light in the next.

A figure steps out of the mirror. It does not crawl or stagger. Its movements are fluid, though what passes for its feet never touch the floor. It is draped in a shapeless cloak of fluttering dark, and rising above it is a blank, staring face. Its mask is now even more deteriorated, a manifestation of its crumbling prison walls.

From behind the mask, something looks out.

It sees the boy, but not with eyes.

From behind its mask it is smiling, but it has no mouth.

It moves to the tattooed boy, who flattens himself against the wall, grim and trembling, the baseball bat in his hands a futile gesture. For if he is to die this night, at the very least he will not die a coward, though he is very much afraid.

But death does not come for him tonight.

Instead,

I do.

The black figure stops when I step forward, blocking her path to the cowering boy. A hissing noise fills the air, containing all her impotent rage. She is strong, the strongest she has been in many years. She has mistaken my inability to prevent Yoko Taneda's death as weakness. Yet she herself has not completely broken free of her seals, and I hold more power over the fate of children.

She snarls, and in her mind I can touch madness. But I have endured my share of insanity, and I stand fast. The towering blackness surrounds me, threatens me, but I force it away with my presence, my will. She did not expect me to be this strong.

For a long time she stands, unable to proceed, and a silent unseen war wages between us. Then she leaps forward, attempting to brush past me to get at the boy. But for all her quickness, I catch her wrist easily with one hand, and

crush

it in my grip.

She shrieks in pain. I hear a startled gasp behind me.

The masked woman knows then that she is not ready.

Not while I am here, defying her at every turn for reasons creatures like her would never understand.

On the teenager's body three seals have been broken; one other seal, stained in Callie's blood, has not yet succumbed. But there is one tattoo still sealed, and this is her flaw.

And so she retreats, step by painstaking step, forced to relinquish ground. She gnashes her teeth at me one last time, and then she disappears.

I believe that I could have destroyed her right then. But the stifled sounds of pain coming from the boy are the reason I do not.

The boy is cradling his wrist, in the same spot I injured the woman. He stares at me, fearful that I, too, have come for vengeance.

Instead, I sit on the floor several feet away from where he still cowers, legs folded underneath me and hands on my lap. I watch him. My physical appearance does very little to redeem my intentions, but it does not take long for the boy to realize I mean him no harm.

"Thank you," he manages to say, still rubbing his wrist, which has begun to swell slightly.

I say

nothing.

Tentatively, he emerges from his hiding place and walks toward where I am kneeling. He hesitates for one long moment and then, with the clumsy fingers of his uninjured hand, reaches out to touch my hair, to convince himself of my corporeality. I let him, though he soon retreats, afraid such action would merit him some offense.

"Why?" he asks.

His is a question ripe with possibilities.

Why, indeed?

For so long I thought that wreaking my vengeance upon murderers and killers was the only path I had left to take, my mind closed to other alternatives. Only now, I discover that preventing the deaths of children has as much potency as avenging them.

For three hundred years, I have rescued countless souls. But I never bothered to learn their names, to understand their hopes and their dreams, to know who they were and what they might have become. To me they have always been nothing more than fireflies that give me brief moments of comfort.

It was never in my nature to be interested in the living before.

I take his hand and examine the wound I inflicted there. It is not in my nature to heal, so instead I press the tips of my fingers along the base of the wound, a quiet apology. I do what he is afraid to do on his own, and lift his palms and let him touch my cold, clammy face. The lamppost continues its solitary flickering, winking at us like a fiery eye. With each flare, my features change abruptly, from young girl

to dreadful spirit

and back again.

Then the light disappears for several seconds, leaving us in darkness. When it finally returns, no longer quivering but shining strongly, I have settled into my former human shape. When I was alive, I had shining dark hair and brown eyes and skin light enough to be considered delicate by some. This is what he sees now.

I am not always a monster.

And when he sees this for the first time, I hear his breath catch in his throat.

"You look…you don't look anything like what I expected."

There is little to say to that statement, and I wait for him to calm down, to break the next bout of silence. He slides to the floor beside me, glancing back at me every so often to assure himself that I do not mind.

"You're a ghost, aren't you?" Then he answers his own question.

"Well, *of course*, Tark. Stupid question. Nothing in the movies ever mentioned anything like this—" The sudden, stricken look on his face quickly tells me he regrets sounding so cocky, still fearful I may not comprehend how he hides his uncertainties behind his banter. "I'm sorry, I didn't mean to sound... I've always been told I'm a smartass."

But I know now that his habit of sarcasm is a part of his nature, just as my malice is of my own, and for the first time in centuries I smile so very slightly.

"My name is Tarquin," he says after another hesitant pause, though emboldened by my reaction. "Tark."

It has been so long since I have heard anyone speak my name or have allowed it to pass through my own lips. In a moment of weakness, I find myself replying, my unused voice issuing from cracked, unmoving lips, my own name tripping on my tongue from disuse.

Okiku.

Oki-ku.

O

ki

ku.

"Okiku," I whisper.

"Okiku. That's a nice name—"

He looks up again, only to realize he is sitting alone on the floor of his room with nothing remaining for company except the moon looking in through the windows, shining and bright.

I have always striven for detachment, a disinterest in the living. Their preoccupation with each breath of air, the brevity of their lifetimes, and their numerous flaws do not inspire sympathy in me. I can plumb their minds and wander the places they frequent, but they hold little significance.

I do not care to remember names. I do not care to recognize faces.

But this one is called Tarquin Halloway.

He has a cousin named Callie Starr.

His eyes are very bright blue.

He is lonely.

It is not in my nature to be interested in the living.

But there are many things, I have found, that defy nature.

CHAPTER ELEVEN

A FUNERAL

Funerals are strange things.

Perhaps it is because I have not had one of my own that their importance eludes me. Ashes fall to ashes, and dust falls to dust whether bodies are buried with full honors underneath the earth or thrown onto the wayside and left to rot. Funerals seem less about comforting the souls of these dearly departed than about comforting the people they leave behind.

Yoko Taneda's funeral does not bring much comfort to the Halloways. The rites are finally concluded on a rainy Sunday morning. The coffin bearing the woman's body is placed inside a large incinerator, and the fires underneath are lit. The emotions on the older man's face are easy to decipher: bewilderment and shock and grief. Tarquin is harder to read. His face is gaunt from exhaustion and trauma that should not have endured in so young a face. His eyes are unusually blank, deep pools of black that stare at the burning coffin and yet also at nothing.

Few people attend the cremation services. Few people in this part of the world knew the woman, and few are willing to look into those flames and be reminded of their own fragility. But the teacher's assistant

no, not the teacher's assistant—

Callie; her name is Callie—

is among those who have come to mourn. She stands apart from the unfortunate family, biding her time to approach. She glances up sharply, sensing she is being watched, and sees me. I am standing several yards away at the other end of the room, the skirts of my dress fluttering in a faint breeze that comes from no clear source. My head hangs low. I do nothing but watch the boy as the coffin continues to burn, and she senses in an obscure way that I, too, have come to pay my respects. A man in front of her takes a step to one side and blocks her view, but once he moves away again, I am no longer there.

When the ritual concludes, people file past the bereaved family to offer small words of comfort. After several minutes of this, the boy becomes discomfited by all the sympathy and finally wanders off, away from the dank soot of the crematorium and out into the foggy day. The girl waits until the crowd around her uncle has thinned, before approaching him.

"I am so sorry, Uncle Doug. How are you two holding up?"

The man accepts her embrace. "Thanks, Callie," he says and tries to smile, though it comes out as a grimace. "Tark's okay— surprisingly, after everything he's been through these last few weeks. The therapist says he's taking things a lot better than…"

He pauses and takes a deep breath. "We're going to take her ashes back to Japan. She grew up in Aomori. Her will asks that Tark and I take her ashes to a small shrine there." His brow creases, and Callie understands his confusion over this unusual request.

"Will Tark be going?"

"We both will be. I'm going to take him out of school for a while. This year's been disruptive enough as it is. We both need a little time to heal. I think that, at this point, it's for the best."

"I'm sorry to hear you're both leaving. I wish there was something more I could do."

"You've done more than enough. I don't think I can ever repay you for saving Tarquin. I…" The man pauses, his face crumpling for a few seconds before remembering himself. "I know you saw her shortly before she…she died. Did she say anything to you? Anything that might be important?"

The young woman hesitates, unsure of what she should say, unsure of how much the man really knew of his wife. "She said that you and Tark must return to the little dolls of Yagen Valley. To her sisters."

The man shakes his head in bewilderment. "I met her when we were both students at Tokyo University, and I know she was born in Mutsu province, where I believe Yagen Valley is located. But I don't know what she means by 'little dolls.' Yoko had a sister, but I'm told she died many years ago. All Mr. Bedingfield—our lawyer—could tell me was that she had some relations in Mutsu, but all he had to go by was an address."

Remembering the news accounts of the crime, the descriptions of the body, and the strewn dolls in that tiny room is enough to send another shudder through his niece. "Do you think it has anything to do with her doll collection?"

The man lifts his hands, helpless. "I don't know. It sounds preposterous. Collecting Japanese dolls is a hobby of hers, but that's not an unusual pastime. I still don't understand." Anger laces through his voice, anger and grief and an inability to refer to his wife in the past tense. "The police aren't being any help at all. They say there was no evidence that anyone was…that anyone was inside with her. The last person to see her alive was the attendant who brought her dinner." His voice breaks. "Why would anyone even want to kill Yoko? Why would anyone do that to her? It must have been one of the other patients at Remney's."

"Uncle Doug," the young woman says timidly, suddenly formal. "Have you ever seen anything unusual around Aunt Yoko? Or with Tark?"

"Unusual? I don't know what you mean by that."

"Have you ever seen…well, strange women around Tark?"

The man stares at her blankly, and Callie realizes that her uncle is ignorant and unaffected by the things that had haunted his son and his wife for so long. "Strange women? Other than the man who tried to kidnap Tarquin, I haven't heard of any other strangers. Did Yoko say something about a strange woman?"

But the young woman is already shaking her head. "No, no, I just thought…it's nothing. Please let me know if there's anything else I can do. Mom sent an email. She says she's sorry she couldn't be here in time."

"She has nothing to apologize for. Send her all my love."

The young woman hugs him one last time, stepping back to allow others the chance to offer their own condolences. She drifts toward the incinerator and watches glimpses of orange fire flickering cheerfully along the outlines of the vault door that separates her from the intense heat inside. *What should I do?* she silently asks herself. *What do I do?*

She does not expect an answer. But from inside the incinerator, where the dead woman's body lies within the flames, come the distinctive sounds of thumping.

The young woman steps back in alarm and glances toward the crowd of mourners. No one else seems to hear the noise.

The thumping begins again, and with it comes a peculiar scratching.

Like something is raking its nails on the other side of the vault door.

Like something is inside with the burning corpse, trying to claw its way out.

The young woman turns and runs, not stopping until she is finally outside the funeral parlor, the light rain falling all around her. She stares back at the building, shivering, afraid that something might have followed her out.

"Callie?"

Despite the wet, the boy sits in some tall grass several feet away, looking quizzically at her. "What's the matter? You look like you've seen a ghost."

"Tark!" she bursts out, unable to respond to his question. "I…I don't know. There was—I thought there was a—something was scratching at the—I think I'm going crazy."

"Welcome to my world." The boy does not sound surprised. He points at the empty spot to his left and indicates that she should join him there. His right wrist is heavily bandaged. "I'm not going back inside, anyway. Too stuffy."

Still trembling, the girl sits.

"You sure you're okay?" he asks.

"I…yes. I should be the one asking you that question. What happened to your wrist?"

"Accident. Nothing to worry about."

"Are you sure you're okay?"

"Oh, I'm peachy," the boy says, a bitter smile on his lips.

"I'm so sorry, Tark."

"Don't be. You're in this mess because of me. I should be the one apologizing. If not for you, it could have been my funeral everyone'd be attending now."

"That wasn't your fault, either, and you know it."

"I know. *She* did it." The teenager said it so softly that she almost missed the words.

"The…the masked woman?"

"Yeah, the…" The boy blinks back at her, surprised. "How did you know?"

"I've seen her, too. There is a woman in black I've seen around you before, back at the…" She pauses, decides it would not be prudent to bring up the unpleasantries of the past, and attempts a different approach. "And there is another woman in white."

The boy nods his agreement, still looking surprised. "Thought I was the only one who could see them both. I was half convinced I was going insane, like Mom."

"Aunt Yoko…I know it sounds odd to say after everything that's happened, but I think she really did love you, despite everything."

"I know that. I just wished she loved me the way a normal mother would have. Like making me cookies or grounding me. Not giving me these."

The teenager stares down at his arms. As before, his long sleeves obstruct the tattoos curling into his skin. In a spontaneous display of trust, he tugs one up to let her see them briefly. The seal no longer moves and twists, and the ink here seems lighter now, half faded into flesh.

"I've been seeing that masked woman since I was a little kid. And I've had *these* for as long as I can remember. Everyone says Mom did it, but I don't really remember how I got them. It's like all my childhood memories before I was five years old had been completely erased.

"I hated these tattoos. I was always picked on by the other kids, and their parents thought I was a freak. Kids would either bully or ignore me, and on the rare instance someone would try to make friends with me…well, weird shit happened. You remember all those dead birds crashing into the cafeteria? That's happened before, in Maine.

"There were other things, too, like decaying smells that come out of nowhere, strong enough that the school had to be evacuated a couple of times. I found a hundred dissected frogs, some still hopping, in fifth-period math once. And there were small earthquakes that only extended out a couple of meters, and nobody could explain that, either. Once at my old school, a piece of plaster crumbled and a host of dead rats came tumbling out, all with their heads cut off.

"And every time, I black out. Every time I come to, I'm somewhere else from where I recall being. It's happened frequently enough whenever I'm around that people started connecting me to all these weird incidents and staying away. Dad doesn't believe that, naturally, being dear, old logical Dad. And word soon got around school that I had a mom in a mental institution, a mom who attacks me before I can even get in a 'hello.' Not exactly the best way to climb up the social ladder."

"But that's awful!" Callie is appalled. "Why didn't you or Uncle Doug ever tell us about this?"

Tarquin snorts. "What, Dad telling you and Aunt Linda I was crazy, or me telling you both I was being haunted by an eyeless woman with a mask, or that I was responsible for my old school almost closing for failing to reach local sanitation standards? If you hadn't told me you could see her, too, we probably wouldn't be having this conversation."

"This isn't something you should be going through alone, Tark. I won't let you!"

Tarquin flashes her a swift, grateful smile. "You're treating me like one of your fourth-graders again, Callie."

"Half my fourth-graders think ghosts are people running around in a white sheet, and the other half think they're some kind of Pokémon."

"Well, she tried to come after me last night. Don't worry," he adds, spotting Callie's stricken expression. "Okiku saved me."

"Okiku?"

"The other ghost. The girl in white. We…she's all right." An odd note enters the boy's voice. "I don't know how much you've seen of her, but she's… Sometimes she wanders around looking like she'd been floating in a river for days, but that night she was… She can actually look kind of *pretty*, you know? Don't know why she doesn't look like that all the time. Maybe it's some unspoken rule about being dead that I'm not aware of."

"Tark, I'm not sure you should be sympathizing with someone like her just because she saved your life," Callie says, uneasy at the remembrance of my dead face, my broken neck. "She might have some other ulterior motive."

"Like what?"

"You've heard about the murder at Holly Oaks, right? They say the victim's face was bloated—exactly like that man who kidnapped you and nearly killed me! I've been doing a lot of research. I've read newspaper clippings dating back dozens of years about men who'd been killed in the same way, and how no one has ever found out who's responsible. They've all been suspected of murdering children themselves, but many of them have never been arrested or convicted for a number of reasons. I think—I think it's *her*, Tark. She's been traveling all around the world, looking for people like them to kill."

Tark merely shrugs at that, and Callie does not like the quick manner with which he dismisses her fears. "Then I'll have to make sure not to go around molesting teenagers of both the handsome and tattooed persuasions, so she won't want to murder me, too, right?"

"That doesn't mean she still isn't dangerous!"

"I don't know. It doesn't feel like that at all. I mean, she saved my life. She saved yours, too! It feels like she genuinely wants to help. And with her around, maybe I can finally stop accidentally killing off people."

"What do you mean by that?"

"There's something else Dad and I neglected to tell you and Aunt Linda. Before we came to Applegate, there was this other boy…" The boy stares down at shoes dug deeply into the damp soil, the dirt obscuring the whites of his laces.

"I've never told this to anyone else before," he says.

"I understand if you don't want to talk about it…"

"No," the boy says, making a decision. "You've seen her, too. I don't like it, but you're in this with me now. Besides, he was a bully. His name was Todd McKinley. But I still can't say that he deserved it. I don't think anyone deserved dying like that."

The words pour out, painting the vivid images I see inside his head.

The bully is a stocky boy of marginal width and height, a menacing memory. Tarquin is younger, frightened. I watch as the bully pushes him against a bathroom door, lifting him high enough that his shoes kick out, barely reaching the floor. But when the bully pulls a fist back to punch Tarquin in the stomach again, the lights go out.

Immediately the older boy begins to scream and does not stop.

It is only after the lights come back on that the other teachers and students arrive to find Tarquin huddled underneath the sink. The bully's legs and arms are scattered across two of the bathroom stalls. His head is found in the toilet bowl of the third, face burned and heavily disfigured.

"People started avoiding me after that, pretended like I wasn't even in the room with them. Everyone thought I had something to do with it, and they were scared. Even the teachers wouldn't look me in the eye."

Callie finds she cannot stop shivering.

"I was glad to leave that school. Everyone thought I was a freak long before that happened, anyway. Never really stopped feeling guilty about it, even if I didn't do the actual killing—like maybe the reason he was dead was because I *wanted* him dead. And then I started seeing *her* more often, the woman in black. When McKinley died, bits of the mask she wears start crumbling—not that she has what you would call a *face* in any normal sense of the word. And when I heard about how Mom died, in almost the same way McKinley did…maybe Mom was right to try and kill me." The boy shudders.

"Don't ever look at her directly, Callie. That thing behind the mask…everything wrong about humanity is hiding behind it. And now it's happened again."

"What has happened again?"

Once again, Tarquin slowly rolls up his sleeve, exposing the rest of the tattoos. The lines of strange writing running up his arm look bleached and worn, as blanched as the seal on his right wrist. In contrast, the seal on his left wrist had not faded like the others had; translucent one moment, dark in the next.

"There's more." Tarquin turns and lifts his shirt partway up. Like the ones on his arms, the other tattoos are also faded, except for one of the two seals at the small of his back that is still an inky black.

"Is it too optimistic to hope that they'll *all* disappear soon?"

She has broken many of those seals, Tarquin's mother had said. And Callie knows that her blood marks the now-sputtering seal on her cousin's left wrist, remembers the hooded woman staring down at her as she lay helpless on the gurney, that evil, decayed face looking out at her from behind the pristine and porcelain doll-like mask.

"Callie, what's wrong?" Tarquin asks, studying her face. "You're as white as a sheet again."

"I'm just—I'm just a little overwhelmed by all this."

"I won't stop you if you don't want to come near any of us after this, you know. I don't want to get you into any more trouble."

"We're in this together, Tark." *I'm in this, too*, she thinks. *My blood is on that seal. Even if I stay as far as I can away from them, she'll still be able to find me. And kill me.*

"It doesn't matter. We're going back to Japan. Dad's company wants to send him to Tokyo because he speaks Japanese, and he wants me along. And we've still gotta bring Mom's ashes back to Yagen Valley, wherever that is."

"I could be going to Japan soon, too."

The boy turns to look at her, and I know the young woman feels it as well as I can. There is something about the masked woman in black that lurks out of the corner of the boy's eyes, though he himself does not know.

"Why?" he asks.

"You remember that cultural studies program I applied for? Japan is on the list of countries I can opt for, if it hasn't filled up already."

"You're not sticking around here to teach anymore?"

"Probably not. I'm getting a little sick of being pointed out as 'the girl in that serial-murderer case.' Anyway, I'll be back in time for college applications."

"What about Aunt Linda?"

"I told Mom about the murder, but not that we were both involved in it—and since Uncle Doug doesn't know her email address, I intend to keep it that way. She's got enough going on in Africa that I don't want to add to her worry. I did tell her about the exchange program, though, and she thinks it's a great opportunity for me."

"I guess it is. Just promise me one thing, Callie. Don't get your-self into any more trouble on my behalf. I'm in enough as it is."

"What, you get into trouble?"

They grin at each other. "What does she want with me, do you think?" Tarquin asks suddenly.

"Who?"

"Okiku, the woman in white. Sometimes I feel like her presence chases the other woman away, but I don't know why she's suddenly so interested in protecting me. One way or another, I'm going to figure out a way to break this curse or…" He trails off.

The girl follows his gaze. For a moment she thinks she can spot me some distance away, outlined against the horizon with my back turned toward them, also watching the remains of the drizzling morning.

Tarquin begins whistling almost absently to himself. It is a familiar lullaby.

CHAPTER TWELVE

GOOD-BYE

"All the other teachers say you're going away," the girl says. "Miss Palmer says so, and so does Mr. Montgomery."

"Yeah, I am." They are sitting on the swings during recess on Callie's last day at Perry Hills Elementary.

"When will you be coming back?"

"I don't know yet. Maybe in two or three months."

"Are you going to Japan so you can make that bad woman go away?"

Callie considers this carefully. "I don't know how to do that yet. But I'll do what I can to make sure that she'll never hurt anyone else."

The little girl reaches over and takes Callie's hand.

"I hope you do," she says, and she is both worried and frightened. "I don't want you to die."

THE WELL

"What's that?"

"Huh?" Callie realizes that one of her fellow tourists named Allison is peering over her shoulder and reading off her laptop screen. Like her, Callie and eight other teenagers on the plane are taking part in the cultural studies program in Japan. Allison, the brunette, is a cheerful and easygoing dark-skinned girl, quick to offer friendship.

"'Japanese ghosts and hauntings?'"

"I just wanted to know a little more about Japanese folklore."

"You could have asked me." The brunette pouts, makes a pretense of being insulted. "I'm the one taking the Japanese studies major in college this fall, you know, and *my* facts won't change every half hour like Wikipedia does."

"Okay, then, Miss Self-Professed Japanese Expert. I've been trying to find out as much as I can about one particular ghost."

"Shoot."

"Her name is Okiku."

The other woman's face brightens. "Oh, *that* Okiku. Of course I know something about her. Most people who study Japanese culture are familiar enough with her legend."

"A legend?"

"You know all those Japanese horror movies that came out not too long ago, like *The Ring*? Well, they're all based on her story. She's the Patient Zero for undead Japanese women with long hair and pale faces, so to speak. As far as the myth goes, she's said to have spurned a nobleman's offer to be his mistress, and in revenge for the insult, he killed her and threw her down a well. Himeji Castle's one of the educational tours we'll be going on, and a place there called Okiku's Well is where the murder supposedly took place."

Callie swallows. "The legend says she broke one of ten plates entrusted to her for safekeeping."

"That's all the nobleman's fault, too. He broke it deliberately without her knowing to guilt her into being his mistress. Men, right? Bastards, no matter the time or place. After her death, they say her ghost still climbed out of the well to count the nine plates and would go nuts whenever she can't find the tenth, which was—I don't know, about *every freaking time*. Someone supposedly figured out how to lift the haunting. Some samurai hid and waited 'til she appeared. As soon as she counted up to nine, he jumped up and yelled 'Ten!' and her ghost disappeared after that. I always thought that was kind of ridiculous. Not to mention it's a horrible trick to play, even on a ghost."

"Was the man ever punished?"

"I don't think so. Japanese ghost stories aren't all that fond of punishing male murderers, for some reason. Double standard, I guess."

"Do you know of any other ghost story where the number nine serves as an integral part of the story?"

"None that I know of. There could be some local stories floating around that never got a lot of international interest. I know for a fact that several are way out of whack. Like there's this little girl who haunts toilets, of all things. And some women wandering around the countryside without faces. Why are you so curious about Japanese ghosts all of a sudden, anyway?"

"It's nothing." Callie blushes again under her friend's scrutiny. "I'm just trying to immerse myself in the culture, and the old stories sound like the easiest place to start."

"Huh. Well, I hope you're still as enthusiastic about it once we get there. There's nothing fun about waiting seven hours for the next connecting flight out of Chicago."

The plane ride is of no consequence to the young woman. While her friend takes quick naps, waking every now and then to grumble about the bad food and the uncomfortable seats (of which the plane has two hundred and seventy-five), Callie wonders about this sudden decision to involve herself in things she has no business in. But at the back of her mind she is aware that she has come too far to back out now. Her cousin is in danger, she tells herself, and so is she.

When the plane finally touches down at Kansai International

Airport, the students duly present their passports and visas, and are soon bowing to a genial, round-faced man who introduces himself as Fukuyama Mori-san, their guide for the duration of their stay in Japan.

"We have a small rental bus waiting." His English is impeccable, though his heavy Kansai accent gives him away. "We will take you to the apartments where you will be staying, so you can unpack and make yourselves comfortable for our first educational tour the next day.

"It is quite fortunate," he continues, as their bus makes its way out of the terminal and onto the main express road, "that the Japanese government and His Majesty, the Emperor, are more than eager to fund grants for students such as yourselves. The earthquake has done very little to improve our tourist industry, though I am happy to say the numbers are increasing again. We will naturally avoid all the places that have been hit by the radiation, but there are so many more sights to see here. From the National Bunraku Theatre to the Municipal Museum of Art in Kobe—"

"Himeji Castle, too?" the girl's friend asks, with a sly grin in her direction.

Mori-san beams. "Himeji Castle, most definitely! It is one of the most magnificent examples of our architecture—we call it the White Heron for the way the whole fortress seems to alight on the mountaintop, just like that magnificent bird. In fact, we will be taking a tour of Himeji Castle tomorrow. If there is anything you would like to ask in the meantime, do not hesitate to do so. I shall answer any questions to the best of my ability."

The ten students are given four apartments, which, in turn, are divided by shoji screens that draw easily across. There are clean futons instead of beds, rolled up and ready for use.

The group enjoys a small dinner at a nearby *izakaya* with Mori-san, who continues to regale them with stories about Japanese history. Callie asks if he happens to know any ghost stories other than those of Okiku's where the number nine heavily figures in, but the puzzled look on the man's face gives her all the answer she needs.

Once they return to the apartment and the lights are extinguished, Callie finds herself lying awake, staring up at the ceiling. Her fears curl up inside her, magnified by the dark.

In the corner of the little apartment, I hang down from the ceiling and watch her prone form and know that she is aware of my presence. I, too, have followed her to this land of ancient secrets and quiet solace. After several hundred years, the taste of my old home, my old country, is sweet in my mouth.

"What do I do now?" Callie whispers into the growing darkness.

I do not reply.

For all I am, I, too, am not infallible.

The tour begins at the break of dawn "to beat the crowds" as Mori-san explains. Nonetheless, when the bus brings them and forty-six other tourists to Himeji Castle, a substantial crowd of people (four hundred and three) are gathered by its entrance, though Mori-san explains that this is a small number when compared to the weekends.

Even from a distance, the white fortress shines in the sun. Several parts of the castle are heavily under construction, and a large tent stretches out over several of the tower fortifications, much to the other teachers' disappointment. Mori-san, however, remains optimistic.

The castle tour guide is a thin man named Tomeo. "These are the servants' quarters," he explains, as he leads them down a long section with numerous doors leading into seventeen smaller rooms. "Each servant's rank in the castle was determined by the room they stayed in. The highest-ranked servant had the room closest to the exit, and each preceding room denotes a servant with a similarly decreasing rank. The inhabitants of Himeji Castle were very particular about their social status, their perceived stations in life, and it shows, down to even the domestic help."

Callie turns her head briefly and catches sight of me drifting into one of the bedrooms farther down the hall. As the guide continues with his monologue, she slips quietly away and enters the room I disappeared into.

It is one of many small quarters in the castle. It is one befitting a humble, unimportant servant.

There is nothing now in the room to indicate its previous owner's preferences or her idiosyncrasies. The bed is bare, wooden and devoid of design, and the barred windows look out into the great courtyard outside, where soldiers once trained under the lord's watchful eye.

Callie looks out the window and does not see them, but I do.

I can still see the clashing of swords. I can still hear General Shigetoki barking orders as he drills the soldiers again and again, until they perform adequately enough to his satisfaction. I can still see the gleam of silver and the flashing of blades. I can still see the quiet young lord who stands before these men as they practice, watching them train long and hard so they can fulfill their purpose: to defend the castle and protect him from enemies foolish enough to assault Himeji.

I can still remember his dark brown eyes and

the way he

frowns a certain way when he is deep in thought. I can still remember

how he throws his head back and laughs when he is in high spirits, and I can still remember how he

sulks for days

when queer moods take him, his flaring temper. I remember how, this creature of dark still remembers, how I remember my heart

racing, this heart that has not beaten in over three centuries. I remember how my heart raced when he took my hand very gently in both his own and said, in his strange and gentle voice—

Okiku,

I will always be in your debt;

that strange and gentle voice, as he turned to his retainer and said—

Do with her

as you will.

With shaking fingers, Callie traces the faded wooden frame, knowing that this was where, several hundred years ago, a girl named Okiku once laid her head to rest.

"The paths inside Himeji Castle were built to confuse invaders," the guide continues, after Callie rejoins the group. "You will notice that the corridors are not built with the same sizes in mind. Hallways lead into secret passages not easily discernible to 'the eye. The stairs are of varying heights so invaders might trip while engaging the defenders in battle. Outside, I will take you to a hall farther on where a whole passageway can collapse with the removal of a single keystone.

"Himeji Castle's builders created these complexities for one purpose, and one purpose alone: that in the event the castle was overwhelmed, its inhabitants would be able to defend its walls long enough for the lord of Himeji to commit hara-kiri. It was considered dishonorable among samurai to be taken alive after being defeated."

For all its outside grandeur, the inside of Himeji Castle is wooden and sparse, nearly devoid of furniture and ornamentation. Empty suits of armor greet the tourists at selected corners as they climb the last of the steep stairs to have their brochures stamped with an authentic Himeji seal. From outside, the *shachihoko*, half-tiger and half-fish gargoyles, stand guard on the castle turrets, their tails lifted in haughty dismissal.

The castle itself is nearly how I remember it, and yet the turning of centuries has saddened me more than I care to admit. What had once thronged with warriors and *daimyos*—great leaders—who discussed and paved the paths to Japan's great future, who held the lives of the people in the palm of their hands, the place that had once housed and protected the man I had once served and

loved,

has now been overshadowed by the hum of tourists, who, in their misguided appreciation, only consider Himeji Castle a memory of the distant, once-glorious past.

By the time the group wanders out of the fortress and into the series of almost labyrinthine mazes on the castle grounds, it is early afternoon. "We have time for one last place to visit," their guide says, leading them toward a large imposing gate and beside it a five-story tower. "This is the *Hara-kiri Maru*," he says, "known as the Suicide Gate. It is here where lords and dishonored samurai were forced to commit hara-kiri, sometimes to atone for their masters' sins. And this is the donjon, the main tower of the castle keep."

"Was this well used for drinking water during a siege?" Callie's friend asks, peering gingerly inside.

"No, nothing of that sort. It was used to wash away the remnants of the disembowelment ritual of the hara-kiri. This is famously known as Okiku's Well."

For a moment, the sun seems to hide behind the clouds, casting the surroundings in a queer gray color.

"This is the well Okiku's ghost is supposed to haunt, isn't it?"

"That's right. It is one of our most popular ghost stories, perhaps second only to the *Yotsuya Kaidan*. There are many different versions of Okiku's legend. The Himeji version is that Okiku was a young maidservant working for the lord of Himeji Castle, whom she loved dearly. She alerted him to an attempt on his life, allegedly by one of his chief retainers. In revenge, the retainer broke a plate from the lord's most prized collection, and Okiku was found guilty of the crime. The faithless lord allowed the retainer to torture her extensively before throwing her body down this well.

"Since then, her ghost rises from it and counts the lord's collection of plates, traditionally between the Japanese witching hours of two and three in the morning. Each time she finds only nine, and each time her unearthly screaming and wailing would wake the lord from his sleep. In time, his health broke from her nightly hauntings. Unable to find peace in death, her ghost is said to haunt the well, even today."

"That's a sad story," the brunette murmurs.

"But true," Callie says, so softly that no one else hears her. She knows that I have gone far beyond the boundaries of my well and have long since sought the greener pastures of other countries, wreaking my vengeance on men still within my reach, those who could serve in the cruel retainer's stead.

Her friend looks down the well and makes a face. "Well, it's too dark to see anything. Let's go take a peek inside the Suicide Tower instead."

She moves away. Before she turns to follow, Callie looks into the well herself—

—and sees a lone woman lying at its bottom, her body twisted and broken from a fatal fall.

Someone hurt her really, really badly, and they put her down someplace that was dark and smelly, like a big hole. Her head went in the hole first before her feet and she died like that, so she got used to seeing everything upside down.

But I am not the Okiku she is familiar with.

This Okiku is clawing at her own face, black bile bubbling up from the wounds scored into her skin. Her mouth is wide and black and hollow, and she is screaming soundlessly, horrid gurgles at the base of her mangled throat, where bone protrudes.

But the most frightening thing about this Okiku are her eyes, as they contain nothing but hollow sockets teeming with black leech-like maggots and look nothing at all like eyes.

It was this Okiku that drowned in this well three hundred years ago, the Okiku I was when I first began my existence as a dreadful spirit, as a nothing-more. This Okiku only remembered

pain

suffering

hate

vengeance.

Time had taught me to temper the malice within. But for a long,
    long

time, I was a great and terrible thing. I was a creature that found pleasure in the ripping. In the tearing.

I am no longer that monster. But memories of that creature still lurk within this well. There are some things that never fully die.

And now, still gurgling, this Okiku begins to climb.

Limbs twisted, ragged strips of kimono fluttering behind her like broken wings, she climbs. She slithers up the wall, brittle bones snapping, she

climbs. Her skin stretches and breaks, hanging down at unnatural angles as her head tilts, loose flesh clinging to the folds of what remains of her neck, and she

climbs. Before Callie has time to react, this Okiku has climbed to the top of the well, reaching out for her with rotting hands, leaping for her with jaws agape.

The young woman turns to run and nearly crashes into her friend.

"Hey, hey, slow down!" The woman laughs. "What's the hurry? We've still got lots of time to sight-see!"

Callie cranes her neck to look behind her, but nothing comes out of the well.

"Mori-san says we're going to see the gardens next. 'You've seen one garden, you've seen them all' is pretty much my motto, but since it's already been paid for, I don't see how we have much of a choice. You ready?"

"Y–yes, I'll be right with you." This time Callie sees the Okiku she is more accustomed to, looking down into the depths of the well myself. Perhaps some of the sorrow and regret is evident on my face when I look back at her, my head bowed in apology.

I am sorry that she sees more than she ought.

I disappear from her view. Callie risks one last look inside the well but this time sees nothing but darkness and hears nothing but the sound of water and the clattering of small stones.

CHAPTER FOURTEEN

LETTERS

I drift from one to the other—first Callie in her small apartment in Kansai, then Tark at the apartment in Tokyo. Their surroundings could not be more different, for Callie lives simply, surrounded by her fellow students' conversation and tatami mats. Tark is more accustomed to luxury, and the rooms he shares with his father are filled with art and opulence.

Some days I watch Callie. I follow her as she attends lectures, plays, tours. I look on as she browses through heavy books, riffles through old pieces of parchment, watches television. Sometimes she knows I am there and lifts her head to stare fearfully at where I stand until I move to leave. There is a wariness to Callie still, a distrust she struggles to hide. I do not blame her.

But much of me remains with Tarquin. The malignance that often surrounds him has retreated, as if my presence alone deters it. I give the creature few chances to resurface. I follow him as he wanders the busy streets, leafing through magazines in quiet cafés, peering into store windows. Like Callie, he is quick to notice my presence, but his reaction is one of welcome. Before long, he makes his overtures to me, bold where Callie is cautious.

"You know what this is, Okiku?" he says, gesturing for me to stand by his side and ignoring the puzzled gazes of passersby. "It's called an arcade game. For a few yen you get to kill imaginary aliens or space monsters for fun. Except this is Japan, so in this game, you play an angry father instead, and you get bonus points for how many things in the room you can destroy by flipping a table up. Child protective services in the States are gonna *love* this game."

"Do you ever get hungry, Kiku?" he might say on another occasion. "I mean, I could buy you a milkshake, too. People leave food in shrines here for all kinds of ghosts, so I'm assuming ghosts actually do get to eat... Does ghost food even exist?"

I do not often understand what he means, but it never seems to matter.

We visit clothing stores, restaurants, parks. He takes me to Tokyo Tower ("The best view in Japan to see modern capitalism hard at work!"), to Hachiko's statue ("Don't tell anyone, but the movie made me cry."), to Harajuku Station ("I know a lot of people here set world fashion trends and all, but that guy looks like he's wearing every piece of clothing his mother owns.").

He tells me to sit by a bench overlooking a small park full of colorful flowers. I am, I feel, understandably reluctant to do so, but he persists. "It won't take very long. I work fast." He sits across from me, takes out his pen and paper, and begins to sketch.

A short time later, he shows me the finished portrait. It is that of a lovely woman gazing wistfully off to one side, admiring the roses in bloom.

I cannot do it justice.

"For a ghost," Tarquin says, teasingly, "you sure do have a ridiculously low opinion of yourself."

I find these short, spontaneous trips with Tarquin

pleasant.

Tarquin and Callie talk frequently in what Tarquin calls *email* exchanges—odd, invisible letters that reach out and bridge the miles that keep them apart. Often, I look over their shoulder as they write, wondering. I had few family members during my lifetime, and delving into Callie and Tarquin's words and thoughts this way, their obvious concern for the other, makes me yearn for something that is no longer my privilege to feel. I do not know why.

Heya, Callie, Tarquin writes,

Japan is officially the most dysfunctional place I have ever set foot in, and I have been inside a mental hospital. Did you know they've actually got a vending machine here that sells used girls' underwear? The Japanese government declared them illegal or something, but I guess that's never stopped a bunch of entrepreneurs from leaving them around. Dad says he's seen others that sell umbrellas, eggs, and for some strange reason, batteries. I'm hoping there's a machine here where you can buy your very own giant robot.

So I almost tried this underwear machine out—just to, you know, see if the thing actually works—but my acute sense of shame finally won out. There are so many other fun ways to dishonor the family name that buying girls' underwear shouldn't be one of them.

Just the other day, I found a salon that specializes in giving girls crooked teeth. And this is considered adorable if, uh, Japanese girls who look like a vampire needing braces are supposed to turn men on. Also, there's a holistic care spa specializing in dogs. I think in my next life I'd like to come back as some rich Japanese lady's labradoodle and enjoy all these spoils. Kinda ironic that most hot spring resorts allow for dogs, but not for people with tattoos. So I guess in this current Japanese social hierarchy we've got Japanese > pets > me.

(Not that I mind too much. I'm not so sure I like the idea of bathing in public, anyway. I know people say communal bathing is a test of how comfortable you are with your manhood and all that other crap, but manhoods should be heard and not seen, thank you very much.)

That didn't sound right. I might have mixed my metaphors up, but I'm sure you know what I mean.

You told me to send you an email as soon as we've settled in Tokyo, and right now we're doing most of our settling in a swanky apartment high-rise at Shibuya that looks like it's been designed by an architect who'd had one too many shots of bourbon.

Tark pauses to glare at the walls of his room, which are covered in seven expensive paintings, each with its own alarming splashes of color.

There's lots of bulging concave art and intricate metalwork that contribute absolutely nothing to functionality except to sit there and look intricate, and there's a table here that can defy the laws of physics to also become a makeshift lounge chair and bookcase. I'm still expecting some metallic female voice to come popping out of the woodwork to welcome me into the future. Also, everything's too polished. I can see my reflection on the toilet bowl lid. (Said toilet bowl also has a bidet. And a seat warmer for the tush. These people think of everything.)

I was expecting to grab some tatami mats, roll out the futons, and pretend it's possible to camp out in Tokyo. As it is, I'm afraid to touch anything because everything looks expensive and breakable, though admittedly this is just the way Dad likes it. The only greenery I've seen so far in this glass dome of technological awesome is a potted plant in one corner, and I'm pretty sure that's about as artificial as everything else in here.

Nobody we've talked to speaks much English, so it looks like I'm going to have to learn a new language soon. Dad says there are more than three thousand letters in the Japanese alphabet, which could pose a problem. There are only twenty-six letters in the English alphabet, and I get into enough trouble with them as it is.

I haven't seen *her* since arriving here, which is always good. But I've been seeing a lot of Okiku…

At this point, Tarquin lifts his head and smiles at me. "Having fun so far?" he asks lightly. I shoot him a puzzled look, but he only laughs and turns back to his laptop.

149

...and as strange as this might sound, she's usually the high-light of my days. Do you think that's a bad sign?

We have this one creepy little kid for a neighbor who looked like he could be the poster boy for every scary movie involving dead children, ever. He went up to me once and asked why "shitai-chan" was following me around. I asked Dad later what "shitai" meant, and he said it meant "dead body."

Like I said, creepy little kid. His parents probably had a blast with that one.

I guess that means something's still following me around. I'd have more peace of mind if I knew what it is.

You in Japan already?

Educational tours and school visits make up the better part of Callie's days, and she only finds time to respond when everyone is sleeping at the apartment she shares. Your emails always amuse me, she says first, smiling as she rereads his letter.

I've been in Japan for three whole days! Except we're in an area called Kansai, which is a part of Japan that's south of Tokyo, and I don't think it's as busy or as populated as I would imagine Tokyo to be. There aren't as many shopping malls and restaurants (so no vending machines with used underwear or doggie spas, thankfully), but there are a lot of other things I bet you won't get to see in Shibuya.

I saw a geisha the other day, maybe only a couple of years older than I am. She had on the most gorgeous kimono I've ever seen, all butterflies and paper lantern lights, and her face was made up in white powder and rouge. She said she just got back from entertaining a client who's an executive at one of the biggest companies here in Japan. Mostly just playing shamisen, which my friend says is a Japanese instrument that's like a guitar, and she and a group of other geisha sang and danced for a bit. Though I imagine their singing and dancing would be much different from what you and I are used to.

I'm helping a friend here named Allison to put together a thesis paper for when she returns to Canada. She'll be majoring in Japanese studies this fall, and her paper's called "The Development of Traditional Performance Arts in Response to Japanese Modernization" with a specialization in bunraku theater. Bunraku, I have since discovered, means "Japanese puppet shows." We've been traveling to a lot of places, including a small island off Honshu, where we watched a few people put on some very elaborate bunraku performances. Some of the puppets cost as much as $2,000! Their clothes probably cost more than all of mine put together.

As for the boy you mentioned, he reminds me one of this one girl I taught back in Perry Hills Elementary. Her name is Sandra. She's probably not as creepy as your neighbor—she's actually quite adorable when she wants to be—but sometimes she worries me.

Just the other day, we went to Himeji Castle. We visited a place called Okiku's Well, which they say a ghost haunts every night when the castle closes to visitors. I'm not quite sure how Okiku was able to leave Japan or wind up in Applegate, but I just had the oddest experience involving her at the well.

It is because spirits do not often choose to linger in their places of death.

Callie starts visibly when she hears, then sees me, nearly upsetting a cup of tea by her elbow. I realize my mistake and, not wishing to cause her more worry, drift past her sleeping companions and fade from view. When she is assured that I will not return, she resumes her typing, though her hands still shake.

I'll tell you more once I get to visit you and Uncle Doug. In the meantime, let's not talk about odd kids and ghosts! How have you been feeling? The program won't end for another couple of weeks, but I've already made arrangements with the Japanese representative to travel to Tokyo instead of leaving with the rest of the students. I'll see you guys then!

The days pass slowly, and a profound change comes over Tarquin. He begins to lose weight. Dark circles form under the hollows of his eyes, and he becomes more exhausted, taking to sleeping more frequently. There is very little that I can do.

Sorry for not replying sooner. I'm feeling tired lately, and I've been sleeping a lot. I haven't been doing much while Dad's at work, just walking around all day and taking in whatever sights I can find. I've been to the Shibuya shopping district, which has an insane number of people at any given time of day, even at night. It reminds me a bit of an organized stampede, like a sea of people rising up to do battle at Prada armed with nothing but shopping bags and a credit card, or something.

I think that's what's been getting me tired. Dad's worried. I can tell because he just canceled two meetings he had to attend so we could go to three doctors who ran a lot of tests but couldn't find anything wrong with me, anyway. They think it's a form of culture shock, trying to get used to being in Japan. I mean, I'm pretty shocked no one seems to know what ketchup is every time I set foot in a McDonald's, because that must be the only reason they don't serve it, but I don't think that's necessarily the deal breaker here.

I even had sushi for the first time today. It tastes a little funny, but it's not too bad. Finding any reason to eat food raw and skip cooking altogether sounds good in my book.

So in summary—no one really knows what's wrong with me, if you exclude the fact that I can see dead people.

Nice to know a little more about Okiku. If I was a ghost I'd be bored haunting the same spot for hundreds of years. I'd try getting into Disneyland since I could get on all those rides for free. Or Las Vegas. Would an underage ghost still be allowed inside a casino, hypothetically?

One other thing. This morning there was a small earthquake around Shibuya—nothing worrying, just strong enough to be noticed. And apparently the seismologists they spoke to for the evening news are puzzled. Japan has an earthquake warning system to let them know about these things in advance, but this earthquake never even triggered it. Only people within a three-mile radius of the apartment actually felt the shocks, which doesn't seem to be normal earthquake behavior. I'm hoping I have nothing to do with this, but it doesn't seem likely.

Neighbor kid was just at the door. He wanted to know why we wouldn't let the woman into the apartment. I asked him what woman this was, but he just shrugged and wandered away.

What is the deal with all these weird, creepy ghost-seeing kids? Exempting yours truly, of course.

Gonna head off to sleep.

He downplays his condition, his humor masking his own worry, and Callie thinks little of it at first. Been eating lots of ramen since getting here, she writes instead.

It's easy to make, and that's good. I don't think we've had much time to cook lately. There are a lot of small affordable ramen shops near the apartment we're staying in, and we've been making use of them a lot. There's one shop in particular called the Oishiya that serves almost the most perfect-tasting ramen I have ever had. Allison says that Oishiya literally means "delicious store," and I can see why.

Are you getting enough to eat, and are you taking some vitamins? (I know I sound old. Shut up.) I don't know much about Tokyo, but the air in the countryside is supposed to be good for your health. You should ask Uncle Doug to bring you around places that won't have as many cars or people, like somewhere outside of the city without all the congestion. From your descriptions of the people in Shibuya, I don't think large crowds make for the best medicine.

As for Okiku, don't worry too much about her. I'm sure she's been around long enough to know what she's doing, even if we don't.

And yeah—that is one disturbing child.

Tarquin's condition worsens as Callie's Kansai tours draw to a close. His father brings him to prestigious clinics, to medical experts. Tarquin is soon spending the night in hospitals, but little about his peculiar malady is known, and his health declines for no discernible reason that anyone can see. Even Tarquin can no longer pretend to himself that all is well.

I officially admit it: something is wrong with me. I keep falling asleep all the time, and I constantly have this feeling like I might not wake up again when I do. No more wandering around Shibuya for me, at least until I get better.

Had the weirdest dream last night. I saw some guy all dressed up like a samurai, throwing Okiku down a well. In my dream, Okiku wasn't the frighteningly dead specter in white we both know and love. She had on that kimono you described for me, the one with the paper lanterns, except it had glowing fireflies on it instead of butterflies. She looked really torn up. Bruises and cuts and worse, and I knew the guy did all those things before he pushed her inside. I remember being so mad at what he'd done to her, like I wanted to tear the guy to pieces with my bare hands, but I couldn't move or speak. And when the jerk looked my way, he suddenly transformed into the masked woman in black which, as you can imagine, freaked the absolute shit out of me. Thankfully, I woke up before I could wet the bed.

And you know something else that's odd? I slept twelve hours today, have been up for only about five minutes—and I'm already sleepy. Been hibernating close to fifteen hours a day now, and while I enjoy being unconscious as much as the next lazy bum, I gotta admit that this isn't natural. Got another doctor's appointment tomorrow for that. Woo-hoo.

Dad says next week should be okay to visit, if you can get away by then.

P.S. Managed a decent conversation with the apartment guard earlier today. I think something might have been lost in the translation, because he's claiming there's no little boy living in the apartment next door. There WAS some kid matching the description I gave who died several years ago, though.

PLEASE, for the love of molasses, get here soon.

A day before the rest of Callie's companions leave Japan to return to their respective countries, Tarquin's father sends her a letter.

Callie—Tarquin has told me about your plans to visit us in Tokyo, and I apologize for the delay in emailing you. Tark's been feeling a little under the weather all week—he's thinner and paler, and I'm worried that the strain of the past few months has finally caught up to him. I've taken him to several doctors, and they're currently running some tests.

I had initially planned to make the trip to Yagen Valley earlier this month, but Tark's illness kept forcing me to postpone. If the tests on Tark come back negative, we'll be heading to Yagen Valley with Yoko's ashes. I think the fresh air might do him a bit of good. We all could use a little rest.

As your exchange program will be ending tomorrow, will you be available to fly out by then? Tark and I can meet you at either the airport or the train station, whichever form of travel you prefer. I have booked two rooms for the three of us at a nearby hotel. (I insist on paying for any expenses for Yagen Valley as well. It's the least I can do, given everything that has happened. I feel that at this point you'll be much better for Tark's health than the doctors or I ever could be.)

Let me know when would be the most convenient time for you. All our love.

Callie's reply is both swift and brief.

Thank you for being so generous! Yes, I'll be available by next week. I'll be arriving at 4:30 p.m. tomorrow at Narita International Airport. Lots of love to you both.

CHAPTER FIFTEEN

BOYS

The boys do not yet know that they are about to die.

Still in their high school uniforms, they watch television. They laugh and tell tall tales and trade stories as the night wears on. They pass around bottles of beer (twenty-seven) that they pour and drink from small glasses (six), and empty instant noodle packages (seven) litter the floor. The room is none too clean, a small and rundown Tokyo apartment no bigger than an average American walk-in closet, but the boys feel comfortable here.

Every now and then, one will excuse himself and leave to use the bathroom at the end of the narrow corridor leading out the room. While the boisterous laughter from his companions continues, he enters the washroom, pushes the dead girl's body away from the entrance with a foot, and uses the urinal, too drunk for the moment to care about the rancid smell and the stink of burnt flesh beginning to permeate through the air, or about the blood splashed against the walls, the red liquid circling the drain, dripping, dripping down the girl's naked body. He zips up, washes his hands like the good boy he's supposed to be, and slides out, rejoining his fellows and leaving her alone in the darkness.

The corpse's arms and legs are severely burnt in several places, her breasts and genitals mutilated. One lifeless eye stares up at the door. The other is swollen shut.

The sixteen-year-old girl is their first kill and still freshly dead. To the boys, she was nothing more than an experiment, a small price to pay for the thrill of taking a life.

The night wears on, and I bide my time. My experiences with Tarquin and Callie do not

crush them take them break them

still the hungers, the malice that bubbles within.

I am who I am.

"What are we going to do with *her*, Hiroshi?" One of the boys, an emaciated-looking teen with acne scars, asks after some time has passed, when they can no longer pretend that the smell does not bother them. "The stench's making me lose my appetite, and she's gonna stink up the house for days."

A tall boy with a shaved head shrugs. "Well, we gotta get rid of her soon, anyway. Get your old man to clean up the mess once we're done, Jo, but we gotta figure out a way to dispose of the body without anyone else noticing."

"There's a small concrete factory just down the block, right?" Another one of the boys speak ups, this time a silver-haired youth with a tiger tattoo on his neck. "We could dump her into one of those cement barrels."

"Get some garbage bags, Shinji," says the Shaved Head, who is in charge. "Tetsuo, Koichi—you guys help him. Jo, go to the kitchen and get some sharp knives. A saw, if you got one. Ya-chan, help him look."

The boys disperse. The acne-scarred teenager and his companion, a boy with a bright purple Mohawk, head downstairs, where an old man and a frail woman sit quietly before a small table, their tea lying untouched before them and slowly growing cold.

"Hey, you," Acne Scars tells his father. "Go find us a saw or something. We need to get rid of the girl."

"Jo-chan. You can't…" his mother begins, pleading, but she is interrupted by the Mohawk. He slams a hand down onto the table, causing the cups to rattle, tea slopping out onto the wood.

"Didn't I say you are not to disagree with us?" he spits out. "Do I have to keep reminding you old fags who I am every fucking time? I'm good friends with people from the yakuza, bitch. One word from me, and they'll slit your throats. Hey, maybe the next time you speak up I might just kill you myself! Fucking old crone!"

Shaking, the father leaves the room and returns with a large circular saw. The mother begins to cry. Their son says nothing.

The boys return to the second-floor landing, where the others are waiting. "Better lend me some old clothes to wear while I cut her up, Jo," Shaved Head says. "I don't want to wash no fucking blood off my shirt."

Acne Scars flips the light switch as they enter the bathroom. The bulb overhead sputters and dies out.

Shaved Head swears. "What the fuck is wrong with the light? Jo, go get a new one."

"Mom only changed it yesterday," Acne Scars whines, but he obediently trots off to look for a replacement. One of the other boys, with unkempt hair and a scraggly beard, turns on a penlight, splaying the beam across the bathroom walls.

"Hey, Hiroshi," he says hesitantly. "I can't find the body."

"What?" Shaved Head grabs the light and shines it around. The girl's corpse is nowhere to be seen. He swears again.

"Who the fuck do you think you guys are, playing pranks on me? Whose fucking idea was it to hide the body?"

"We didn't do it, Hiroshi!" a boy with glasses protests. "We were with you this whole time."

"And we were downstairs looking for the saw," Mohawk adds hastily, for Shaved Head is known for his foul temper. "I swear, Hiro, we never moved the body!"

"Well, I want you all to start looking for it soon, because I'm losing my patience. Where the hell is Jo with the light?" Shaved Head flips the light switch on and off again, then punches his fist into the wall, his frustration apparent.

"Go look for Jo," he barks out. "And see if the old farts downstairs had anything to do with this."

His companions rush to carry out his orders, leaving him scowling at the small, smudged mirror in the bathroom. "Idiots," he mutters, smoothing out his rumpled shirt collar.

And stops. A peculiar dark spot in the mirror is growing slowly in size as he looks on, though the darkness makes it difficult for him to see clearly. Frowning, he scrunches up his eyes and draws closer to the mirror, trying to determine what this is.

The black spot increases, spreading across the mirror's surface like an ugly paint splotch, until Shaved Head can barely see his own reflection.

"What the hell?"

Two discolored arms shoot out from the mirror, and it is only from reflex that Shaved Head is able to throw himself away from their reach, hitting the wall behind him hard instead. He gapes at the mirror, where a long-haired woman's head begins to push itself out. From underneath her hair, eyes like twin black holes bore into the now-terrified boy's face, and from her wide, scarred mouth she gurgles low.

"Shit!" Shaved Head bursts out of the bathroom, skidding across the narrow hallway. "Jo!" he yells. "Shinji, Tetsuo! Where the fuck is everybody?" He runs toward where he last saw the boys, halting beside the room they previously occupied. The room is empty, though the TV still plays. A strange screeching noise makes him stop in his tracks.

A variety show program is on: Japanese comedians on a game show. But the television screen occasionally flickers into a different image—barely more than a few tenths of a second at first, but growing longer each time, until Shaved Head finds himself looking into the face of the murdered girl. Her skin has been warped from burn marks and stretched over her horrific skull.

Blood begins to spill in rivulets down the walls of the room, soaking through the curtains. At the same time, something drops from the ceiling behind him and hits the floor.

They are Purple Mohawk and Tiger Tattoo, both unrecognizable if not for their brightly colored hair. Their legs are twisted behind them, like all bone had been leached from their limbs. Tiger Tattoo is obviously dead. His features are an ashen gray, tongue lolling out. But Mohawk is still dying. Half of his face is bloated and swollen, and he flops helplessly across the wooden carpet, a gutted fish out of water.

"Hlllp," he croaks. "Hiroshhhhhhi."

Something

gurgles

by his side. Shaved Head sees me standing on the ceiling for the first time, watching him with my pupil-less eyes and my hollow, open mouth.

Shaved Head flees, ignoring his dying friend's garbled pleas. He races through the hall. "Tetsuo!" he screams. "Koichi, where the hell are you guys? Fuck!" He shoves open the door leading into a small storage room but steps back, frightened, when two of the other boys come tumbling out.

Both are also dead. Scraggly Beard's eyes are rolled so far into his head that only the whites are showing, and Glasses suffers from deep claw marks that rake across his face and tear through his clothes. Like the Mohawk, both their faces are putrefied, decomposing.

"Hiroshi!" Acne Scars is running toward him, and Shaved Head is relieved to find him still alive, though every inch as terrified as he. "What's going on, Hiro?" he wails. "Yasushi-chan's dead! I…"

His voice trails off as he stares down, shocked, at the two other dead boys at his feet.

"There's nothing we can do for them now! We gotta get out of here!" Shaved Head dashes down the stairs, Acne Scars tripping and stumbling behind him. The old man and woman are still sitting by the table, though they are now clinging to each other, terrified by the commotion.

"Did you do this to fuck around with us, you old prick?" Shaved Head grabs the old man's shoulders and shakes him hard. Acne Scars loses his balance, landing noisily on his rear by the small wardrobe. The old woman shrinks back, covering her eyes with her withered hands. "Answer me!"

But the old man does not look at him. He is looking over his shoulder at something that drains all the blood from his face.

Slowly, Shaved Head releases the old man and turns.

The wardrobe door has opened, and another pair of arms encircle Acne Scars' neck. Half my body leans out, my hair brushing against the boy's cringing face.

Acne Scars' gaze is locked onto Shaved Head's, realization dawning alongside terror on his ugly, pockmarked face.

"Hiroshi," he whimpers. It is the last thing he will ever say.

I

dr

    ag

him into the confines of the wardrobe, the door sliding shut behind us.

Shaved Head sinks to his knees. The tiny wardrobe rocks hard against the wall as terrible screams ring out from within. For some minutes these continue, until they finally cut off abruptly.

For a long moment there is silence.

Then from inside the closet the scratchings start up again. So do the low, gurgling sounds.

Shaved Head runs past the frightened couple and snatches a metal baseball bat.

"I'm not afraid of you!" he shouts. "I'm gonna kill you! I'm gonna kill you!" Crazed, he brings the bat down on the sides of the wardrobe with a strength that belies his lanky build. "I'm gonna kill you! I'm gonna kill you!" Over and over again he attacks it, and the cheap wood slowly gives way.

He smashes the doors, battering at the wardrobe until the frame shatters from the repetitive blows, until the hinges break free and the plywood splinters to reveal that there is nothing inside the wardrobe but clothes—not Acne Scars, not anything else. But the boy does not stop. He grabs at the sides of the wardrobe and pulls it down onto the floor, destroying it completely.

Shaved Head pauses, panting heavily from his exertions. "Did I kill it?" He wheezes and then starts laughing hysterically. "Hahahaha! I killed it, didn't I? I killed it! Sonofabitch!"

He levels a kick at what remains of the wardrobe, still giggling maniacally. "You're not going to get me, bitch," he crows. "You're not going to get me!"

But his laughter falters when he hears the scratching again

despite everything to the contrary—a scratching coming from underneath the broken planks of wood.

Frenzied, like a man possessed, he begins to pull the heavy pieces of timber away from the floor. When most of the wood scraps have been discarded, he burrows into the pile of clothes, pawing through them until something snags his foot, forcing him to land on a body.

It is the body of the dead girl, arms folded across her naked chest.

Her eyes open. Her bloodied hands reach up to cup either side of the boy's cringing face, almost caressingly. She even smiles.

But those same bloody hands tighten inexorably around him, and Shaved Head is yanked forward into her waiting mouth.

It is hours before either of the old couple can be persuaded to leave their table. But when the aging man sweeps the strewn clothes away with a trembling hand, there is no trace of either the boy or the dead girl.

It is her decision.

Unlike other souls that I have saved, this girl does not glow, does not rise up to the sky. Unlike with other souls, the prolonged violence of her death has warped her into the creature of malice standing before me.

Unlike other souls, she is much like me.

She has not changed. Her skin still bears the marks of the

torture she went through in the moments before her death. This is clear in the lacerations on her body, in the ruins of her face. Like me, she has exacted her revenge against her tormentors, but her loss of innocence from such actions ensures that she cannot cross into the light. Like me, she cannot leave and is instead doomed to wait forever on dark shores, straining for glimpses of stars.

She understands this. Still, a smile curves along what is left of her mouth. She bows to me, for even spirits can understand gratitude, and turns to leave, the night soon swallowing her up.

I should not feel sorrow that she chose of her own volition to take the same path I now walk. But I do. I am beginning to understand that there are better things than retribution.

I, too, leave this terrible place, this little apartment of bodies. There are no souls to save here. Anything worth redeeming left this place many, many years ago.

Instead, I wait for the break of dawn. I find an empty shed washed clean from the stink of the living and slip back into hibernation. Briefly, I contemplate returning to Tarquin's apartment instead, but I do not. For the first time in as long as I can remember I feel unclean. Impure.

Uneasy.

So it is in this little shed in Tokyo that I wait for Callie to arrive.

Tarquin Halloway and his father are there when she steps out into the waiting area of Narita International Airport in Tokyo, and Callie is stunned by how Tarquin looks. She expected him to look sick from their email exchanges where Tarquin recounted his health, sometimes deprecatingly, but nothing prepared her for the hollowness of the tattooed boy's cheeks or the pallor of his skin or the feverish brightness of his dark eyes. Despite his now-frail condition, there is energy to the teenager still, and he closes the needed distance to exuberantly throw a thinner arm around Callie's shoulder.

"I know what you're thinking," he says, his smile a mere ghost of what it could have been. "I look fantastic."

"Oh, Tark!"

He laughs at her fears. "Don't worry. I'm a lot stronger than I look. But I'm glad you're here, cuz."

"He's been growing worse every day," his father tells Callie later, as he drives the rented car into the thick of Tokyo. Tarquin is nestled against warm blankets in the backseat of the car, fast asleep. In spite of what he says, his burst of enthusiasm exhausted him quickly. "I'm at my wit's end what to do. I've been to several different doctors and they've run two dozen tests, but no one seems to know what's been making him sick."

It is the woman in black, Callie knows, but she does not tell the father this.

"I've gotten two rooms at the Garden Rose Hotel. The hospital is only a block or so away, so we can be there quickly, in case one of the doctors calls again."

After unpacking, Callie heads to the room across from hers, where she manages to wake Tarquin long enough to spoon hot chicken soup into him, while his father conducts business with his mobile phone. By the time he is done, Tarquin has drunk most of the nourishing meal, in between halfhearted protests that he could feed himself without her assistance, and fallen back asleep.

"He sleeps most of the time now," his father says, worried. "They have the results of his most recent blood test, and they still haven't found anything wrong with him."

"Maybe it's not as serious as it looks," Callie says, trying to be encouraging, though she knows the deceit of her own words.

"I hope so." The man sinks into a nearby armchair. "God, I'm tired myself. I've been running around Tokyo all day, settling Yoko's affairs and trying to finish the rest of my work in between talking to doctors. I've got several meetings with Mitsubishi and Itochu in the next few weeks. I don't think I've had more than a few hours' sleep since arriving here."

"Maybe a rest in the countryside would help both of you," Callie suggests.

"Yes. Whenever he feels better, Tarquin pores through every guidebook and map of Aomori we can find. I think it'll be good for him, too. Thank you again for coming with us. Tarquin's been looking forward to the trip."

"Did Aunt Yoko have family there?"

"I'm a little fuzzy on that myself. Yoko never talked much about any relatives she might have had. I know that her parents died before we'd even met, but if she had any other siblings or cousins, other than the older sister she mentioned, I'm as much in the dark as you are. She never liked talking about her past, insisting that she was done with that part of her life."

The man gestures, and Callie sees with a start that the urn bearing the ashes of Tarquin's mother stands atop one of the room's dressers.

"Yoko mentioned in her will that she wanted her ashes scattered at the Chinsei shrine near *Osorezan*. I've never heard of the place. I've asked a couple of people, but the closest thing to a temple that they are aware of is the Bodai Temple on the Osore grounds. I suppose we can always ask some of the locals at Mutsu once we get there."

The man's phone rings and he excuses himself to answer. As he talks, Callie steals across the room to gaze down at the small urn on the dresser. She wonders briefly how Tarquin must feel, traveling with his mother in this macabre manner.

"I don't know what I'm supposed to do," she tells it softly. "I don't know what I can possibly do. But I promise to do whatever I can to help protect Tark."

She turns away, back toward the room.

Something rattles behind her.

Callie looks back just in time to see the lid slide off the urn, dropping with a noisy thump onto the carpeted floor. From inside, a jumble of hair rises out of the opening, inch by slow, protruding inch. As she watches, horrified, a drooping eye emerges from underneath that matted hair, and then next, a gaping mouth. It is

Yoko Halloway's head

peering up, and Callie claps a hand over her mouth, stifling the urge to scream. But the dead woman's eyes seem every inch as pleading, a peculiar desperation in that bloodied face. Her torn lips move wordlessly with an entreaty that Callie neither hears nor understands, before the head falls out of the urn and hits the floor, rolling toward her.

"Callie?"

The girl jerks back into the reality of the room, only to find Tarquin's father peering down at her anxiously. "Are you all right?"

In the older man's presence, there is nothing out of the ordinary. The seals on the urn's lid remain perfectly in place. Yoko Halloway's head does not stare up at her from the floor.

"Are you all right?" the boy's father asks again.

No, Callie thinks. *No. I am not all right.*

CHAPTER SIXTEEN

MUTSU

The journey to *Osorezan* comes in stages.

From the Tokyo station, they take the Shinkansen train to a place called Hachinohe. After the hustle and bustle of Tokyo, a certain kind of quaintness seems to settle around this little city. The faintest smell of brine permeates the air.

Tarquin had been sketching all throughout the train ride, his papers filling with small scenes of rural life. Fishermen hauling in the day's wages and the busy and noisy throng of markets are captured in strokes of his pencil. Rather than become fatigued by the train rides and the constant switching of stations, the teenager appears more energized than when he was in Tokyo, and he takes shorter, quicker naps each time.

"You're really good at this, Tark," Callie says, going through his works. "Oh. Is this…?" She holds one up, where he has drawn a simple sketch of a dark-haired, solemn-looking girl, wearing a kimono dotted with fireflies.

"Did that one this morning." Tarquin flashes her a sheepish

grin. "I'm not *obsessed* with her or anything like that. But when you told me about that geisha with the butterfly kimono, and then that dream I had—I couldn't get the image out of my head."

They spend half an hour stretching their legs and pay for packed *obento* lunches from a nearby convenience store. Inside, the clerk is watching television, turned to an English-speaking news channel. Callie does not listen at first until she realizes there is something unusual about the day's report.

"We've received word that police discovered four bodies this morning in the San'ya ward of Tokyo in what they describe as 'horrific' deaths by persons currently unknown. Police have confirmed earlier reports of the victims appearing to have both been drowned and also severely mutilated, making it one of the worst murders in Japan in the last several years.

"All four were students at a local high school. Authorities are searching for two other students last seen with the victims and still missing. No other details have been forthcoming, but we will provide updates as soon as we receive official statements from the police superintendent."

The victims appear to have both been drowned and also severely mutilated.

The *obento* store owner sighs. "Youths nowadays," she says sadly in heavily accented Japanese. "Not what they used to be."

Trembling, Callie can only nod.

They switch trains and board the Aoimori Railway, which Tarquin's father explains will take them to Noheji next, an even smaller town than Hachinohe. Winters here are long, broken only by short, cool summers, and a faint chill blankets the area, though it has yet to snow. From here they take one final train ride to Shimokita. Callie balks at the exorbitant fees Tarquin's father pays each time, but the man is unconcerned by the expense and assures her she owes him nothing. As the train leaves the station, Tarquin persuades his father to explore the train further with him. Invigorated by the new sights, the boy has color returning to his cheeks.

Callie declines the invitation. She is unused to the constant motion of modern locomotives and wishes to remain in her seat to recuperate. As they leave, Callie stares out the window as the scenery changes from woodland to green space to farmland and back again, watching people work at their fields harvesting rice (fifty-eight) or herds of cattle grazing at will (seventy-nine). From a distance, the diminutive shapes of small fishing boats pass (forty), silhouetted against the sparkling waters of the bay.

She turns her head and sees me on the seat before her.

I have never been to the northern part of Japan, but something in the rustic countryside, the sway of thatched roofs, and the endless fields is more familiar to me than the gray stone skyscrapers and the artifice of color in Tokyo. This reminds me of

(home)

the life I once led.

Perhaps because of this sense of calm, I do not appear to her as a dreadful *onryuu*, a massless thing of hair, of torn cotton and skin. Instead, I look out the window from my seat as a young girl in a simple homespun kimono. My hair is coiled in a bun, and the darks of my eyes are now a soft brown, the whiteness of my face now a palette of pink flesh. There is a marked contrast between the hideous appearance of an apparition that I have worn for so long and the simple normalcy of the girl I once was and whose shape I have now resumed, however briefly. I say nothing for the moment and continue to watch trees and rice paddies pass as the train hurtles on, waiting for her to make the first move.

"Your name is Okiku, isn't it?"

Without looking back at her, I nod slightly.

"The same Okiku from Himeji Castle?"

Another nod.

She says nothing for some time. I imagine that conversing with the dead is always difficult for the living.

"Did you kill those boys that were in the news today?"

I smile.

"Why are you doing this?" She knows the answer but seeks to hear it from my own mouth.

There is a long silence before I surprise even myself by speaking with a wistfulness I thought I had lost and could no longer feel.

"I loved my lord," I say in a voice barely above a whisper. It is not an answer to her question, but it is something I have wanted to say out loud for so long, and the truth of those words comforts me.

"Did you kill all those people because of him?"

"I am a servant. I had a simple life. A happy one. I contented myself with loving my lord without hope of return. But he betrayed me to his retainer, and in that moment, I realized I had wasted my life loving an undeserving man. I died with regrets. But I could not leave."

"Tark's been sick for a while now… Was that your doing?" The accusation in Callie's voice is apparent.

I turn to look at her then. "No," I say, a little angry that she would presume to think this. "I would never hurt him."

She is quiet again, acknowledging the truth in my words. "What can I do to help you?"

"There is nothing you can do. There is only me."

Another drought of silence.

"I take from them," I finally say again, and the strength of my anger surprises me again, "because they do not deserve life."

"Why do you help us?"

I finally turn my head to look at her. I do not know what she sees looking back. Calliope Starr is a strange girl, to be willing to face me when anyone else would have feared. But I have often found that people are strange because they have something most others lack. "Because I do not wish to see you or Tarquin come to harm. Because I…"

I trail off, unsure of how to explain other than this: I have no definite reasons, except that I do not want him or his cousin to die. Instead, I look down at my hands.

Callie swallows. "But I don't know what to do. All I know is that Tarquin was used in a ritual to bind some…some *ghost*, and the secrets to undoing that ritual lie in *Osorezan*. But I don't know what to do. I never asked to be a part of this."

"Do you believe he deserves life?"

The young woman is taken aback. "Of course!"

"Then we are not so different, after all."

Another pause.

"I am sorry if I frighten you," I say, puzzled by the sudden hesitancy in my voice. "I am not used to...*this*. I do not often commune with the living."

Callie blinks at me, then unexpectedly starts to laugh. "I apologize," she gasps. "It's just...well, with us, it's usually the other way around."

She giggles again. I do not quite understand but attempt to smile. Perhaps it is not a smile that she sees in my face, for she immediately sobers up.

"There's...there's something else I want to know. Why couldn't you protect Yoko from that other woman—the woman in black?"

She shrinks from the sudden shift in my expression, the black stealing into my eyes, the way my skin now seems to sag and bloat, and the hair that begins to once more curl across my face, shrouding my cheeks. It is not a pleasant sight to watch a young girl turn into one of the dead. I do this not because of any mistake on her part, but because I remember that I have unfinished business with the creature in black, the spirit that seeks to hurt them. And when I speak again, it is nothing more than a hiss as my true self looks back out at her.

"I am sorry. But Yoko is not my

territory. She is not my

    hunt."

"Here you go, Callie! We found a nice old woman peddling snacks and we scared her into selling us some stuff. Here's some Meiji chocolate and something called a noodle sandwich which is, apparently, literally a sandwich with noodles in it. Since *you're* the noodle expert, you're the one that gets to eat it."

Tarquin and his father are back. Callie does not need to look my way to know the seat before her is empty.

Five hours after departing from Tokyo, changing trains twice along the way, they finally arrive at the Shimokita Station in Mutsu, but by then dusk is already settling in. At this time of day, the station holds fewer people, and so the woman stands out. She is dressed in a pleated, ankle-length red skirt and a white *haori*, a kimono jacket that is two sizes too big for her. Her hair is tied back in a loose ponytail. She is still very young, perhaps only a little older than Callie.

"You are Mr. Halloway?" she asks in perfect English, smiling. She bows low. "And you must be Tarquin-kun. My name is Kagura. We have been expecting you."

Tarquin's father is surprised. "We never told anyone we were coming."

"We were very good friends of Yoko. We heard of her death from your lawyer some weeks ago, and we have been expecting your arrival ever since."

That means she must have been waiting every day at the train station for nearly a month, Callie thinks, and feels intimidated by the strength of the woman's patience. "My name is Callie. I'm Tarquin's cousin," she says, feeling how absurd the statement must sound, but the woman accepts this without further question, bowing low to her in acknowledgment. When she lifts her head again, however, her eyes travel over Callie's form with a peculiar curiosity, a slight frown crossing her face before it disappears quickly.

"I'm afraid that there are only four buses departing for *Osorezan* daily, and the last has already left. Fortunately, my sisters and I have a small house on the outskirts of town where we can spend the night. If you will follow me?"

The town of Mutsu is even smaller than Hachinohe or Noheji. The woman leads them to a small house far from the central square, dipping into the edge of town. At her request, the group takes their shoes off before entering and follows her into several comfortable-looking rooms with several screens. She tells them that these are to be their rooms for the night.

"While we do get substantial visitors to Yagen Valley, few of the locals, much less the tourists, are aware of the Chinsei shrine," she says in an apologetic tone. "My sisters and I prefer to keep it that way."

"I've certainly never heard of it. Yoko never mentioned it to me before," Tarquin's father agrees.

"Then I must apologize on Yoko's behalf. She is merely following the old ways, the traditions built around the utmost secrecy. We have done so for many years."

"What about your sisters?" Callie asks with some hesitation. "Will they be joining us?"

"My other sisters are currently tending to the shrine, and they are not comfortable leaving it for long periods of time. Dinner will be ready in an hour. In the meantime, you are more than welcome to explore. Mutsu is not a very big place."

"I've spent the last couple of weeks holed up in bed," Tarquin says later, once they have finished unpacking. "I'm gonna go and have a look around."

"You aren't strong enough yet, Tarquin," his father warns.

But the boy only grins. "You worry too much, Dad. Didn't the docs themselves tell you that there's nothing wrong with me? You're right, Callie. All of this fresh air is making me feel like my old awesome self again."

His father finally relents, and Tarquin sets out. The man begins another series of phone calls, and Callie helps the woman prepare for dinner. She is now dressed in a kimono of somber blue and wards off all of Callie's offers to help, laughing. "It is not customary for a host to allow her guests to assist in dinner preparations. But I would appreciate the company." Her thin, slight fingers slice carrots and meat with the expertise of a chef's.

Every now and then, there is a knock at the door, a voice calling out for Kagura. Each time, the woman briefly abandons her task, taking a small parcel from the cupboard before greeting the caller. "Specially prepared medicine my sisters and I make," she tells Callie, "a sovereign specific, a general cure-all for many forms of ailment."

Her patients are both numerous and varied: first an old man suffering from advanced rheumatism, next a young mother with a sleeping child, then a group of fishermen, followed by half a dozen fresh-faced students. "I suppose it works, which is why many ask for it," Kagura says modestly after seeing the last of her customers off. "I am a *miko*—a shrine maiden. As are all my other sisters. In many small towns where people still believe in the old ways of living, *mikos* like us often serve as the resident medicine women."

"You speak English very well."

"I am the only one of my sisters who can speak it at all, another reason why I was chosen to wait for you. I may not look it, but I have also studied at university." The *miko* lifts her head to look at her, and the same compelling curiosity is back in her gaze. "You are a very unusual girl, Callie-san."

Callie is taken aback by her frankness. "I am?"

"It is not every day that I see anyone, much less an American, with an *onryuu* following her around."

"What is an *onryuu*?"

"It is a kind of *yuurei*, a dead spirit stranded in this world and unable to leave. An *onryuu* is the most powerful kind of *yuurei*—one fueled by vengeance, able to harm the living."

Callie freezes. "You can see her, too?"

"I am aware of her presence, have been since I first saw you at the train station," the *miko* says. "I see her now on the ceiling, standing just over your right shoulder." Callie turns but sees nothing. "I say it is an *onryuu*, yet I feel no hate from her. That is why I say you are an unusual girl. Or perhaps it is an unusual *onryuu*. The young boy, Tarquin-kun, is afflicted by another spirit, but one who is decidedly more dangerous."

"How are you able to see her? Who are you?"

The *miko* sets the knife down. "Shrine maidens nowadays are a far cry from what they were once known for throughout Japan. They still perform ceremonies and offer to tell people their fortunes, but no longer do they dabble in soothsaying or speak for the dead. My sisters and I are a dying breed. We are *kuchiyose miko*, among few still following the old ways. We serve as mediums for the deceased, and so our second sight is strong. Tarquin's mother, Yoko, was one of us before she married his father."

"Yoko Halloway was a *miko*?"

"I was only nine years old when I last saw her, but I believe Yoko Halloway was a devoted wife, a kind mother, and a beautiful woman both inside and out. But once upon a time, Yoko *Taneda* was a *miko* and an exorcist. She was the best of us all—a very strong one, capable of weathering the malice that most dead spirits bring. Her spiritual abilities were second only to…"

And at this the *miko*'s voice trails off. She takes the knife again and resumes her slicing.

"There was one other *miko*. One who surpassed even Yoko Taneda in terms of skill and ability. She could succeed in the most difficult of exorcisms, those that could kill weaker shrine maidens." Her voice grows soft. "And then, unfortunately, she died."

She shakes her head, resumes smiling. "You must not let me

ramble on so, Callie-san. I was only a child when it all happened, but my *obaasan*, the head of the Chinsei shrine, will be able to answer your questions more succinctly than I can."

"You're not afraid? Of Okiku?"

"So you even know the *onryuu's* name." Those soft brown eyes are on her again, but the *miko* somehow looks sad. "As I have said, Callie-san, you are an unusual girl, but I do not mean this in a bad way, and I apologize if I offend you by saying so. Sometimes it is better to be a little unusual every now and then than to be common all the time." Then she sighs and will say nothing more of the matter.

The guests find the boiled eel served at dinner delicious, and Tarquin's father decides they should all turn in early for the night. "It's not like we've got much choice, anyway," says Tarquin, who is eager to rest but does not want to admit that his quick expedition into town has sapped his energy. "Practically everything here's closed for the night."

But Callie cannot sleep. A few hours later, she rises from her futon and crosses the room, careful not to wake the others, and hopes that the crisp evening air will soothe her troubled mind.

She is not the only one awake in the little house. Kagura the *miko* is out in the small garden, once more dressed in her traditional *haori* and *hakama* skirts, socks painted green by the grass and wet from the dew. She is kneeling over a small *Jizo* shrine, and in her hands she holds a doll not unlike those that Yoko Taneda once collected. She places this before the small shrine, murmuring under her breath. Callie stands half hidden behind the shoji and watches her, unsure of whether to interrupt.

What she does not expect is the sudden rage of wind that hurtles through, as if threatening to blow down the house and everyone inside it.

It comes like a screech of sound, an inhuman wail. To Callie, it feels like a sudden hurricane has set down on top of them. She shrinks back inside, clutching at the wooden frame of the doorway, trying to keep from being sucked outside into the howling winds. The *miko* is unaffected, weathering the gale without difficulty. Her long hair billows out behind her like a dark sail, as patches of stone and soil fly past. When a large rock rushes too close to her face, she calmly lifts a hand and plucks it from midair.

"Begone," she says, like an unnatural tempest is of little substance.

Something forms within the violent gusts. Callie expects this to be the face of the masked woman, but instead it is an unfamiliar face—a beady-eyed man with a quivering chin and a long face, nearly skeletal in its shape and form. He opens his mouth and bays like an angry wolf, but the *miko* is unmoved. She raises the tiny doll.

"Begone," she says again.

The face in the wind twists in anguish, as if struggling against another unseen force. Finally, it gives one last shriek of despair before it dissipates completely. The rest of the swirling winds sweep toward the doll, seem to settle on it, and disappear.

The *miko* sits back and sighs.

"It is a small imp, a demon of little consequence," she says without turning around. "A malicious spirit, but more one who looks fearful than one who should be feared. Tarquin-kun attracts its attention, one of the reasons why he has been falling sick in Tokyo. The ghost living inside him has weakened his energy and makes him more susceptible to possession than others. And in Japan, there are far too many ghosts wishing for such an opportunity.

"The *onryuu*, your Okiku, has a different kind of malice in her, more powerful, but one she modifies to a nobler purpose. And she is strong. Very strong. This strength enables her to leave her haunting grounds and move freely about. She has wandered around the human realm as a spirit for far too long, and it will take more than this simple exorcism to set her free, though I suspect she has become too accustomed to this existence to do so willingly."

"Exorcism?" Callie asks, shaken by the fact that the *miko* knows she is there, though the latter does not seem angry.

"It is what we do at the Chinsei shrine. It is a very old technique passed down for generations since Emperor Temmu's time. We exorcise wandering *onryuu* by trapping them inside the bodies of dolls such as these."

Callie gasps. "But…that was how Aunt Yoko…"

"We are saddened but not surprised. Yoko herself sent us a letter telling us what she planned to do, of the ritual she performed on the night of her death. It was a rash decision and very dangerous. She had none of the usual precautions in place. But I suppose she felt she had little choice left." Gently, the *miko* sets the doll back on top of the shrine. "But it is not your Okiku who was responsible for her death, though she is a terrible ghost in her own right. I do not know what binds her to this plane, but perhaps it would be impolite not to ask."

Then the *miko* addresses me directly. "Have you come here to harm us, *onryuu*?" She asks, her brown eyes intent on my face. Callie turns toward her in surprise but still does not see me.

I watch the *miko*. There is great strength in her. Though she is still very young, in time she could be much more.

"Have you?" she persists.

I shake my head, amused by her boldness.

"It is unusual for those like you to involve themselves in human affairs. So why do you come here? Is it because of the boy?"

I lift my head then and meet her searching gaze with a determined stare. I do not respond, but she understands. A grudging smile appears on her lips.

"I see. He *is* rather special, isn't he?" She turns away. "An *onryuu* with a conscience, *kami* help us. I agree with your uncle, Callie-san. It shall be a long day tomorrow. You must rest."

She glides inside. After one last look behind her, Callie hesitantly follows suit, leaving the doll atop its little *Jizo* shrine, moonlight shining on its strange, porcelain skin.

I wait until they are gone before picking it up and turning it over carefully in my hands. Its eyes stare back at me with a strange combination of hatred and helplessness.

CHAPTER SEVENTEEN

FEAR MOUNTAIN

There are only fourteen tourists on the bus as it navigates the slopes leading up the mountain, though the view is one most consider breathtaking. Halfway through the trip, the bus stops by a nearby mountain spring, the driver encouraging the visitors to sample the fresh water. Tarquin has regained most of his health. His eyes are no longer bright from the feverishness that accompanies most sicknesses. He has resumed his habit of regaling his fellow travelers with outbursts of sarcasm. His father is pleased. "We should have done this sooner," he admits to Callie. "Maybe all he really did need was some good, fresh air."

But the *miko* does not share the same opinion. "*Osorezan* is a holy place," she tells Callie quietly once the man is out of earshot, aware of the father's ignorance of the disease that truly plagues Tarquin. "It is one of the three most spiritual places of Japan. *Osorezan* serves as a *shintai*—a place where powerful spirits called *kami* are believed to reside. It is enough to suppress most spirits' malice, if only temporarily."

But *Osorezan* itself does not look like a place associated with holiness. A landscape of black coal rocks and charred soil is what first meets their eyes. The air smells strongly of sulfur and pitch, and the mountain itself is not a mountain at all, but a series of strange peaks that jut out from the barren wasteland. Where other places may have piping hot *onsen*—hot springs—these only contain bubbling pits of more sulfur. The wind howls through much of the region, like spiteful demons calling out to one another, attracted by the fresh smells of humans that enter their lair.

"It is not so bad!" the *miko* says, amused at seeing the looks on the others' faces. "*Osorezan* literally means the 'mountain of dread,' for it is a place where ghosts are said to stop on their way to the underworld. The Japanese people have a very high regard for their ancestors and for *kami*—they believe that everything has a spirit, and that these must also be properly honored by the living. How we view hell is much different from how you Americans view it."

"Is there any way we can visit Japanese hell without a sense of smell?" Tarquin asks, holding his nose.

Only one man-made building of note is found here—what humans call the Bodai Temple, surrounded by several sulfuric hot springs that smell even more strongly of rotten eggs. "The river beyond it is called the Sanzu"—the *miko* points—"our version of your Styx river. All visitors must cross the red bridge over it to gain access to the temple. It's runoff from a lake called the *Usoriyama*. Do not bathe in it, though. The waters may look inviting but are actually quite poisonous, and no living thing thrives there."

Small *Jizo* statues adorn most of the paths. People leave tiny bibs, pinwheels, and other simple toys along these stone figures.

"This place is called the *Sai no Kawara*," the *miko* says next, "the Buddhist purgatory. These statues are to honor those children who die before their parents, and you will find many offerings like these here."

Piles of small pebbles are also found along the paths beside the statues. The *miko* explains these are made by spirits of dead children who, unable to repay their parents in life, are now doomed to constantly build these small mounds of stones until prayers are made to comfort their spirits.

Despite the pervading smell, Bodai Temple itself is an unassuming shrine, its importance rendered irrelevant by the strange world outside its doors. A few of the locals are lighting four candles inside a small shrine that contains the teeth of the dead (Callie draws back in alarm upon being told this, while Tarquin leans forward eagerly), and the incense that wafts through the air is a tangy contrast to the other smells of dank and death.

Beside the temple is a small red pool that the *miko* says is called the Pond of Blood, guarded by more imposing statues and dead flowers. A small woman, wizened and hunched, totters about the grounds, murmuring, "I understand it now, I understand it now," to herself like a small mantra. She smiles vaguely at the visitors, at the Halloways, and at Callie. She smiles at the *miko*, and then at me, and then at the large eyeless stone figures draped in scarlet and yellow aprons, guarding the bloody pool. "Yes, yes. That must be it. I understand it now," she says. "I understand it now."

We spend a few more minutes wandering about the temple. Besides the Halloways, there are three more tourists who quickly leave, perhaps repulsed by the sulfur and the disquiet of the place. Intrigued by the small statues and unaware of their significance, Tarquin's father stops to start up a conversation with one of the priests, and the *miko* joins him.

But Callie sees me standing around the side of the temple, watching her and waiting.

She rounds the corner and follows in my footsteps, and it is here that she sees Tarquin and the man. He is in his mid-sixties, with brown, doughy skin and eyes like a frightened weasel's. He is darker than most Japanese, from days spent under the constant sun, and his knuckles are knobby, fingers pudgy. He is kneeling before several more stone statues in the area, this time eyeless figures draped in miscellaneous cloths of forbidding scarlet and black, and he is rocking slowly back and forth. To those who do not truly see, it looks as if he is kneeling before Tarquin and begging. The boy himself appears grave. He sees the dead children and knows what must happen.

Like him, Callie also sees them for the first time. Two young boys cling to the old man's shoulders, and another lies chained at his feet. They are no more than eleven years of age, and their faces are as worn and as tired as the obese man's, the imprint of their prison years stamped over their listless faces, their dull eyes.

It is here that I make her understand.

The old man shrinks back again when he sees me, but people

like him are more accustomed to the ancient tales of old ghosts and older vengeance. He sees his fate standing before him, and he knows it is a price he must pay. While he was once wild and untamed in his younger years, when he killed these children for the thrill and the sport, in his old age he now wrestles with the horror and the guilt of what he has done, and the fear of what is to come. He comprehends that he has been living on borrowed time ever since, and when he turns to face me, the dread and the terror is on his face, but with it also a quiet relief, an acceptance.

As Callie watches, terrified, I

approach him. The man says nothing, but merely holds out his hands in supplication as he sinks to his knees before me. I reach out only

once,

and my form envelops his, my hair wrapping around his cringing face as I take him. It is in places like *Osorezan* where guilty men repenting of their old crimes come to wait for the end of their life or to wait for one to take it on their behalf.

Finally, the mangled, bloated body slips out of my grasp and sprawls at the foot of one of the figures. Callie cringes at the familiarity of his terrible, staring face. Tarquin says nothing, and his face shows little else but determination. He understands, quicker than his cousin, the sins the man has committed and the necessity of his punishment, however repugnant to human eyes.

But the children are free, and now they are gathering around me. Their faces are tired yet expectant, knowing their own peculiar form of purgatory has finally come to an end. Callie gasps when they begin to glow, and I gather them in my arms as best as I can, once more closing my eyes and surrendering briefly to that inner warmth.

When I open my eyes again, I am surrounded by glowing balls of light where the three children had once stood. There is fearful awe on Callie's face.

Unafraid, Tarquin walks to where I stand, stepping into this circle of fireflies. He touches one, wonderingly, with a finger, but it immediately shies away, bashful even in this form. He turns his attention to me. As he has done before, he touches my cheek tentatively with his hand and looks directly into my face.

"I'm sorry," he says.

I smile at him. Then I raise my hands,

and the balls of light respond, spinning slowly around my arms and the tips of my fingers until they are set adrift on their own, soaring lazily up into the blue autumn sky.

Together Callie and Tarquin watch them rise, higher than the farthest-flung kite, watching them become little specks of morning stars until the last of the clouds hide them from sight, leaving nothing else but the two of them, the now-desiccated body on the ground, and me. And when the last of them disappear, I turn away and vanish as well.

"Why did you say that?" Callie asks Tarquin, a little later. "Why did you apologize?"

"I don't know. I think I'm just sorry she has to keep cleaning up after other people's mistakes all the time."

There is no one else in sight at the temple by the time they return. The old woman continues to putter about the place, every now and then resting a hand against another of the statues, greeting them like they are old friends. "I understand it now," she repeats herself. "I do. I understand it now."

I wonder what it is that she understands.

Yagen Valley is a few hours' hike away, along a small, unused road where no buses will go. The tourists along the road are even sparser at this time of year than at *Osorezan*. Two small hamlets are all that make up the population at Yagen. One is the *Oku-Yagen*, and the other is the unpopulated *Yagen-Onsen*. The *miko* says they are traveling to the latter.

"But the guidebook says *Yagen-Onsen* is uninhabited," Tarquin's father says as he consults his guidebook.

"Are we camping out?" Tarquin asks, stomping his foot on the hard ground and looking uneasy at the prospect.

The *miko* only smiles.

Callie is nervous. Perhaps, after all, the grinning *miko* is not who she says she is. There is little evidence that the *miko* knew Tarquin's mother beyond what she claims, and yet they have embraced her words as the truth. This suspicion is also apparent in the father's face, but unlike Callie, he is unaware of my presence, of the comfort Callie draws at knowing I am close by, my soundless feet padding after theirs. Only Tarquin seems unfazed, pushing on eagerly as we leave the forest path and trade it for the uncertainty of the woods.

"I'm not sure we should go any farther," the father begins unexpectedly, but what he is about to say next is silenced when the *miko* calls out joyfully, "We are here!"

A smaller shrine is nestled farther into the thick of the forest, where no clear trail marks its location to outsiders. The only other visible landmark is a small well that stands beside it.

From inside, a few women emerge. Two are older than the *miko* by at least ten years, but the third is at least thrice as old as the oldest shrine maiden, though she stands straight and tall despite her weathered skin and her long, white hair.

"Kagura," the old woman asks in Japanese, "are these the Halloways?"

The *miko* kneels on the rough-strewn trail and bows, her forehead touching ground. "This is Douglas-san and Tarquin-kun, *Obaasan*. And this is Tarquin's cousin, Callie-san."

The old woman moves along the path. Though her steps are sure, she walks slowly and with a limp. When she reaches us, she surprises everyone else by reaching out with her thin, frail arms and clasping both sides of Tarquin's startled face, kissing each cheek and whispering in more Japanese, though the words are simple enough that her short time in Japan has taught Callie to recognize their meaning.

"Welcome to the Chinsei shrine, little Tarquin-chan," she whispers, "Welcome to Chinsei."

CHAPTER EIGHTEEN

CHINSEI SHRINE

The shrine is larger than it looks from the outside. The wooden floor is carefully swept and the furnishings austere at best, though the place can accommodate five more people easily. There is no indication that anyone else visits the shrine, located as it is within these forests unspoiled by paths.

But the dolls terrify the visitors as they enter the shrine.

Like those in Yoko Taneda's room, they are everywhere. They stare down at the three from glass cases made in every conceivable size and shape and form.

(One doll, two.)

They are dressed in kimonos of varying colors and designs, some with hair done in a complicated coif, while others have hair left loose and flowing. Tarquin makes a strange sound and steps back, while Callie is unable to stifle her gasp. The old woman looks amused and rattles off another fresh string of Japanese.

"I apologize if our dolls make you feel uncomfortable,"

Kagura translates for her. "We use these dolls for most of our rituals and exorcisms."

"My wife used to collect dolls very much like these," Tarquin's father stammers.

"She was one of us, your wife. The Taneda sisters were two of the greatest exorcists of their generation."

"You must be mistaken. My wife is no exorcist."

(Twenty-five dolls, twenty-six.)

"There are many things your wife neglected to tell you." The old woman sounds disapproving. "Yoko was always a dutiful student, but her decision to marry and leave us came as a surprise. And then there was that business with Chiyo."

She shakes her head and makes a small psshing noise. Callie wonders why the name sounds familiar.

"Dad"—Tarquin's words come slowly, unusual for him—"I remember this place."

His father and Callie stare at him. "But that's impossible," the man says.

(Ninety-one dolls, ninety-two.)

"It is not impossible," Kagura translates for the old woman again. "What I am about to say might sound fantastic to you, Halloway-san, but I speak the truth. Little Tarquin has been here once, many years ago. His mother brought him when he was only two years old."

"I remember her mentioning that she wanted to take a trip with Tarquin once while I was away on business. It was the last time I saw her before she…she…"

198

(One hundred and eighty-three dolls, one hundred and eighty-four.)

"Before she went insane," the old woman finishes for him. "I remember you, Tarquin-chan, though you do not remember me. You were very well-behaved. Many of my other sisters babied you incessantly during your stay. If we'd only had the foresight to know what would happen to your mother, we would have asked her not to bring you at all." The old woman sighs. "We must hurry, though, to ensure that you do not share the same fate."

(Three hundred and six dolls, three hundred and seven.)

"What do you mean? What's going to happen to Tarquin?" his father asks in alarm.

A knowing look passes among all four *miko*. "We have heard of your young son's sickness." The old woman is being deliberately misleading. "We know that the doctors in the city will not be able to heal him with their modern medicine. But we are gifted in the old ways, and we would like to try."

Tarquin's father, a stronger believer in these modern medicines than in tradition, looks unconvinced by this, but he does not wish to sound ungrateful. "Tarquin's a lot better than he was in Tokyo," he does concede. "I don't see why we can't stay for the time being. I am thankful for any help you can give."

(Five hundred and sixty-two dolls, five hundred and sixty-three.)

"My name is Machika. This is Saya, and Amaya. You already know Kagura. You are all free to stay for as long as you like in our humble home. Yoko's family will always be welcomed here."

"If you don't mind," Tarquin says, still staring at the dolls, "I'd like a room where there isn't anything soulless looking back down at me, for a change."

Much to his relief, the guest rooms hold none of the seven hundred and seventy-seven dolls of the Chinsei shrine. There are seven more futons laid across fresh tatami mats, and one small wooden table. The other *mikos* do not speak English, either, though they smile frequently and appear eager to assist. Tarquin's father hesitantly gives Yoko's urn to the old woman, Machika, who accepts it with peculiar sadness and regret. "Dear Yoko," she murmurs, "if only you had listened."

She turns to place the urn reverently on one of the larger altars, while the other *mikos* stand silently and say nothing. Some time later, Callie watches as they chant and toss handfuls of Yoko's ashes into the thick foliage that surrounds the small shrine, and she wonders how many dead shrine maidens cover this tiny clearing.

It soon becomes clear that the Chinsei shrine is self-sufficient and has little reason to interact with the other locals. The *mikos* show them their garden, where small herb and vegetable patches satisfy their requirements for food, as meat is not consumed inside the shrine, much to Tarquin's consternation. For other basic necessities, the *miko* Kagura explains, she is often sent to nearby *Oku-Yagen*, or even to Mutsu when supplies in the nearby hamlet are lacking, as they sometimes are. The *mikos* spend their days cleaning the shrine and gathering at certain hours of the day to chant sutras to cleanse both body and spirit. They do not mention the woman in black or the *onryuu* in white as Kagura had, and Callie wonders if only the younger girl possesses this ability while the skills of the older shrine maidens have grown weaker over time.

The next two days are spent in pleasant inactivity. All the *mikos* dote on Tarquin, who is uncharacteristically embarrassed by all the attention, much to his father's and Callie's amusement. They are invited to partake of the hot *onsen* springs. Tarquin and his father go first. When they return, it is Callie's turn.

Kagura and another one of the *mikos* named Amaya accompany the girl on her first visit to the hot springs. "There are three open-air *onsen* in all of Yagen Valley," Kagura tells her as they begin their twenty-minute walk. "The *Meoto Kappa-no-yuonsen* is the only one that offers dressing rooms and showers for visitors. It costs 200 yen, but from the Chinsei shrine, it will take nearly an hour's walk to reach, and another hour to return. You would be tired and exhausted by then, and this would negate the bath's soothing effects.

"*Kappa-no-yu* is the second *onsen* and free of charge, though there are no changing rooms. The third and nearest *onsen* is where we will be headed. No one has thought of giving it a name, perhaps because they wish it to remain as unspoiled as its surroundings. But we have always called it the *Chinsei-no-yu* among ourselves, for we are its most frequent customers."

Chinsei-no-yu is exactly how the *miko* describes it. There is a view of the nearby rapids, but no enclosures or rooms to change in. Kagura and Amaya show little inhibition, eagerly shedding their clothes while Callie, blushing furiously, gingerly follows suit. Among these springs, it seems, visitors are required to shed their modesty as well as the rest of their clothing before stepping into the water.

"Do not be so shy," Amaya encourages in Japanese, and Kagura translates for her friend. "You must rid yourself of all your Western modesty when you come to our hot springs. To embrace the Japanese culture is to follow in the customs of the Japanese at *onsen*. There is nothing to be ashamed of."

Finally stripped down, the three girls enter the hot springs. Callie gives a soft little sigh of contentment the instant her skin touches the water, the constant worries and concerns plaguing her during the last several days melting away upon close contact with such comfortable heat.

They sit in companionable silence for fifteen, perhaps twenty more minutes, simply luxuriating in their baths. "I'm afraid there is another reason we have asked you here," Kagura finally says, breaking the lull. "Douglas Halloway-san does not believe in talk of spirits and rituals, and *Obaasan* fears that the more we talk of what we do, the earlier he will leave and take Tarquin-kun along with him. That we cannot allow to happen. If the boy leaves Yagen Valley, he will soon wither away and die."

Callie suddenly feels cold, despite the hot water. "What can I do to help?"

"You feel differently, do you not, Callie-san?" Kagura asks eagerly. "That is why *Obaasan* has instructed us to bring you here, so that we may explain about Chiyo without fear of being over-heard by Douglas-san."

"Chiyo," Callie echoes, remembering. "Mrs. Halloway mentioned her once."

"She was our sister, a *kuchiyose* like us," Amaya says, Kagura translating quickly. "But she was Yoko-chan's biological older sister, her true *oneesan*. You must wonder how we are able to support ourselves, living in such a lonely place where few people pass through." Callie nods. "We make medicine from the herbs we keep in our garden, and Kagura goes into town to sell them. But there are also many who still believe in the old ways, and there are those who are still afflicted by the old curses. When people become possessed by the demons and spirits that abound, they come to us."

"What do you mean by 'possessed'?"

"The Japanese believe that everything has a spirit." Kagura takes up the tale. "Mountains, trees, even the smallest of stones. When funeral rites are performed poorly, the spirits are unable to move on into the afterlife. They return to the family and loved ones they left behind, often to haunt them. Sometimes the deceased takes possession of a favorite item of theirs during their lifetime, and sometimes they can even possess a family member or a close friend. Sometimes they can physically harm a person or, in rare instances, kill. All *onryuu* are capable of this, though their methods may vary. When this happens, their victims come to us. We expel the spirits and transfer these demons into our dolls as a substitute."

Callie stares at her. "Do you mean to say," she asks slowly, "that the dolls in the shrine all possess spirits?"

Kagura is reassuring. "Not all spirits we exorcise are necessarily evil. Many are simply lost souls, confused by their deaths and unable to move on, and we help guide them on their way. The *Obon* is a festival celebrated every October to honor our ancestors, and at this time every year, we cleanse the possessed dolls by burning them through another special rite. By doing so, we release their spirits back into the underworld. Until then, we serve as their caretakers."

"But…but the spirit haunting Tarquin…"

"Yes," Kagura says sadly. "Her name was Chiyo Takeda. Among us *miko*, she was the most powerful. Her specialty lay in exorcising the most vindictive of ghosts—the evil spirits who have come specifically to do harm to the living. But sometimes dolls cannot contain the fury of the worst of these demons. So she began using her own body as a sacrifice.

"For years she was successful. Her own spirit was strong enough that she was able to house these ghosts within her without suffering the consequences until *Obon*, where she would then successfully purify herself of them. But she grew too proud, Chiyo-sama did. She boasted that she could trap even the King of the Underworld himself. *Obaasan* tried to talk her out of saying such foolishness, but she was unrepentant. She thought herself capable of handling anything."

Kagura closes her eyes. "And then the nightmares began. She had

204

them almost every night, and she became prone to sleepwalking. She nearly walked into the Ohata rapids once and would have died, had Yoko not followed her out and saved her. Her personality began to change, too. Chiyo-sama had always been very gentle and compassionate. Now an uglier side of her surfaced. She would abuse many of the younger *mikos* and physically hurt them.

"When *Obaasan* found her cutting the heads off some of the small squirrels and birds around for sport—the Chiyo we knew loved all living things and would have died before she allowed them to come to harm—she knew that they could not wait for the *Obon* festival for Chiyo to be purified. I was only nine years old when it happened, and still I remember it clearly. I remember her madness." Kagura shudders.

"There was Chiyo, squatting in the dirt over some poor eviscerated pigeon. She cared very little for her appearance by then, and her hair hung in tangles around her face, her eyes starting out from her head. She was like a demon herself."

The *mikos* fall silent, remembering. Callie shifts uneasily.

"The older sisters staged an exorcism to force the spirits out of Chiyo and into a doll especially reinforced to contain them," Kagura finally says. "It was a disaster. Not even the strongest, holiest doll we had could bear her taint. I was too young and was therefore forbidden to attend the ritual. But from my room I could hear her, and I could hear some of the *mikos* who had been driven mad by her. That terrible, terrible laughter…" She, too, shivers.

"After some time had passed, *Obaasan* entered my room, quite pale and drawn. All she could tell me was that Chiyo was dead, and that the demons plaguing her had finally been subdued, but at great cost. They had been naive, she said, to believe even the strongest of dolls could substitute for Chiyo. When demons have experienced a taste of a powerful human vessel like Chiyo was, dolls are nothing to them.

"Poor Yoko was married by that time but aware of Chiyo's growing decline. She insisted on coming to the shrine that day, and Tarquin came with her. When the ritual went wrong, she had to act quickly. None of us were pure enough or strong enough to become the next sacrifice—no one but her own son, Tarquin-kun. The more innocent the vessel, the stronger its ability to contain. Yoko sacrificed him to prevent Yagen Valley from becoming a place haunted perpetually by the ghosts and demons Chiyo had unleashed. But to have brought Tarquin-kun along, knowing full well that the ritual could fail... Perhaps she herself knew it might come to that."

Again she falls silent. Only the soft bubbling of the hot springs mars the quiet.

"That's horrible," Callie whispers, aghast.

"So you can say that Tarquin saved us all, and that is why he is treated the way he is by the others," Kagura says with a small smile. "Yoko tried cleansing him at the *Obon* festival, but Chiyo's spirit did not leave. Perhaps it was the guilt she felt that drove her mad, that drove her to attempt to kill her own son. As a last resort, one can purge a malevolent spirit by killing the human vessel it possesses."

At the look on Callie's face, Kagura quickly adds, "We do not intend to kill Tarquin. But innocence is lost as one grows older, and the spirit that was once Chiyo is now fighting to break free of him. *Obaasan* says that we must act quickly, sometime within the next few days, if we are to rid Tarquin of her malevolence forever."

Amaya says something in rapid-fire Japanese. Kagura responds in kind, and the two argue for a few minutes while Callie sits across from them, feeling uncomfortable.

Finally, Kagura shakes her head and turns to her. "Amaya-chan also wants to know about the *onryuu* that has been following you around."

"I don't know much about her, only that her name is Okiku. From the old Japanese legend?"

Amaya is nodding, looking satisfied. She speaks again.

"Amaya-chan can see her, too, as well as I can. She also does not feel any enmity coming from the *onryuu*, which we both find odd, but I suppose that is not uncommon with long-lived spirits. We believe that objects become personified after one hundred years of existence. They begin to have their own thoughts and feelings, and are venerated as *kami*. It is the same with ghosts—they become stronger, the longer they exist in the mortal plane. If this is truly the Okiku of the legends, then she has existed for more than three hundred years. It is fortunate she appears to be more benevolent than others that come to mind."

"On some other occasion we would try to appease her ghost, but Tarquin-kun's ritual must take priority." Kagura hesitates. "You are more than welcome to leave before it takes place, if you wish. *Obaasan* feels that you ought not to be involved in this for your own personal protection. She thinks it is unfair for you to be here and to put yourself in danger for something that does not truly concern you."

"Tarquin is my cousin," Callie says. "And I've seen the woman in black myself. If my presence can help in any way, then I would much rather be there."

The two *mikos* watch her, this time with newfound respect. "You are a very brave woman," Kagura says. "If I had a choice myself, I would choose to run." She looks over Callie's shoulder directly at where I am standing and nods to acknowledge my presence. I incline my head but do not move.

"*Kami* willing, we might survive this yet."

CHAPTER NINETEEN

EXORCISM

Pressing business summons Tarquin's father back to Tokyo. The head *miko*, Machika-*obaasan*, is alarmed when she hears him making plans to leave to return to the city. "But we have not finished yet," she protests. "Tarquin-kun has been doing very well since arriving here, and I do not think it will be in his interest to return to Tokyo, where his health may take another turn for the worst."

Tarquin's father pauses. He does not want his son's unusual sickness to return, for doctors to worry and prod and run tests and find nothing wrong. Here in Yagen Valley, Tarquin has continued to steadily improve. Surrounded by the adoration of the other *mikos*, he seems happier here than he has ever been in Tokyo or in Applegate.

In the end, Tarquin's father appeals to Callie. "I know that this is an imposition on you, but would it be possible for you to stay with Tarquin for the next few days? There's a business merger I need to oversee, and I'll return as soon as that's finished."

Much to his surprise, Callie is amendable to the idea, assuring him that he would not be forcing her to do something that she is already set on doing. "I like it here," she says, a bright smile on her face even as her stomach churns over what the next few days might bring, "and it's such a nice change from the city. I'd be glad to stay here with Tark."

"Thank you," the man says with a faint smile. He looks around the shrine, perhaps realizing for the first time how little he knew of his wife and how little he knows his son. "Take good care of him," he says unexpectedly, a strange note entering his voice. "I never seem quite able to, myself."

"That's not true, Uncle Doug," Callie says, startled.

"Not in the way I should have, perhaps." He takes another glance at the room. "I didn't really know Yoko, did I? I wish she'd trusted me enough to tell me about this part of her life."

"Dad?" Tarquin has stepped into the room. "You're going back to Tokyo?"

His father nods. "Don't get Callie in any trouble."

Tarquin rolls his eyes. "Yeah, 'cause that's all I'm usually good for."

"No," his father says quietly but with unusual firmness. "I don't always say it, but I've always been proud of you."

The words throw Tarquin off guard. His face is a mosaic of expressions: surprise, gratification, embarrassment. "Sure, Dad," he says awkwardly, though the grin on his face is genuine enough. He gives his father a quick hug. "Don't be getting yourself conned by those Japanese businessmen in Tokyo," he says, and both his father and Callie laugh.

Finally the man leaves, if still a little disquieted by the uneasy feeling there is something here that he is missing.

The *obaasan* is in good spirits. "This will give us all the time we need to finish the ritual," she exhorts after Tarquin's father has gone. She is optimistic for a reason, for she believes this ritual will succeed, unlike others that have gone wrong before.

Kagura takes Callie aside some time later. "This is how the seals were made," she explains, selecting one of the dolls—the same doll Callie had seen her use by the Jizo shrine in Mutsu. She pulls the kimono sleeve up, and Callie is stunned to discover that it bears the same inked tattoos as on Tarquin's skin.

"Every one of the dolls you see here has been hand inked by us." Kagura turns the doll over and lifts the kimono over its back. Like Tarquin's, more of the tattoos dot its sides and back. "To break this seal one must hate." She touches the first of the seals on the doll's back, then the other. "And to break *this* seal, one must respect. To break the seals on the left and right wrists, one must know fear and friendship. To break the seals across the chest, one must know love.

"On the dolls these are merely symbolic; on humans, much less so. Every day we take the dolls out and inspect them. If we see any one of these seals growing faint, we know that they have been compromised, and we perform another ritual to reinforce them or transfer them to another."

"Can't you do the same for Tarquin?" Callie asks, but the *miko* shakes her head.

"Human sacrifices are different. Dolls have always been sterile

211

and unchanging things, but humans are not made the same way. To perform a repurification on a human sacrifice might harm more than it can repair. I have seen the seals on Tarquin-kun. I know that four of the five seals have faded. When the last seal crumbles, the poison inside him will be freed. So much blood has already been spilled for this that we cannot wait to allow *her* to seek more."

"Blood?" Callie feels sick.

"To break each of the seals, another kind of sacrifice is required. The blood of people slaughtered must be placed against the seals to weaken them, and with each break she becomes more powerful. Whenever Tarquin feels frightened or angry, the malevolence inside him is at her strongest and can even control his body to some extent. What is the matter, Callie-san?"

"It's nothing," Callie says hurriedly, her heart pounding as her hand drifts once more to trace at the unseemly scar on her finger, a permanent mark of her very own seal.

"What's this?" Tarquin enters the room, curious. The *miko* shows him the doll, and he winces.

"Would you like to hold it, Tarquin-kun?"

"Wouldn't that be dangerous for me?" He speaks in moderately broken Japanese, one of his many growing attempts to practice the language.

"The seals are in place. It will cause no harm, that much I can promise."

Tarquin takes the doll, holding it by the hem of its kimono so it dangles in the air before him. "This is kinda creepy, Kagura-san.

Why are its eyes so black? Most of the other dolls' eyes don't have any color in them."

"It is because this one is already possessed by a spirit. It is the spirit's eyes that you see, looking out at the world."

Tarquin nearly drops the doll. Hastily, he shoves it back into the *miko*'s arms. He is trembling a little. "This is why boys don't play with dolls. Now if you don't mind, I'm going to go and freak out in the next room."

A day after Tarquin's father leaves, there is an unexpected development. Voices call out from somewhere in the woods, and one of the *mikos* heads out to greet the new visitors. "It is a possession," she reports once she returns, and her words set the other *mikos* off in a tizzy of activity. The *obaasan* becomes businesslike, barking out orders that the others scurry to perform. Unsure of how to assist, Callie and Tarquin sit and watch, fascinated.

Kagura heads out into the garden and returns bearing fresh clumps of sweetgrass and sage. Amaya moves from room to room, setting candles around the shrine in large, concentric circles, lighting each in turn. Incense is added to the small altar, and soon the air is filled with its sweet, smoky scent. The other *miko*, Saya, sprinkles rock salt everywhere before setting up *ofuda*, strips of paper bearing sutras, against the walls and shoji screens.

The *obaasan* takes one of the dolls from the glass display. With quick precision, she slits its body in half, emptying out the cotton balls stuffed inside it. She replaces these with grains of white rice, stuffing the doll before sewing it shut again with red thread. Next she brings out a large stone knife and begins cleaning it with hot, steaming water.

"We are ready," she says, and the *mikos* view this as the signal to bring the possessed in.

It is a little boy, perhaps only seven years old. He is twitching uncontrollably as he is brought in by his worried parents and other concerned relatives. His eyes constantly roll into the back of his head, and his mouth spits horrible, snarling obscenities. Even Callie and Tarquin, who do not understand the words, shrink back at the venom bubbling from the froth of his lips.

"Lay him down on the floor," the *obaasan* commands, and this is promptly carried out, though the boy now screams in agony. Each *miko* holds a limb in place to prevent him from sitting up or crawling away, as the *obaasan* dangles the doll above the boy's head and chants in a long, sonorous tone.

Though the sun was shining only moments ago, a dark cloud quickly passes over the little shrine, over the whole of Yagen Valley. Something that sounds like thunder rumbles through the Chinsei shrine, and the boy's howls grow louder. The boy's parents, now looking very pale, clasp their hands together, mumbling prayers of their own.

For nearly half an hour, the boy twists and writhes in pain, alternating between uttering long frightful shrieks and cursing the *obaasan* in a deep, guttural voice that a seven-year-old should not possess. A small earthquake besets the building, earthenware rattling, the ground shifting and settling. The old woman is unmoved by these threats and continues her long litany until finally the boy begins to weaken. His arms and legs begin to tremble less, and his head rolls against the floor. Finally, he takes a long, deep breath, exhales noisily, and falls silent.

The *obaasan* keeps the doll hovering atop his face for several more minutes after the boy has fallen unconscious. She places it on the ground beside him and picks up the knife.

And just as suddenly, the boy sits up, knocking the knife from the *miko*'s grip. The young child's face is twisted, almost a poor imitation of a human's, little slits of teeth showing through an abruptly wide mouth. His eyes bulge, a bulbous black pair starting out from his head. With one loud, inhuman shriek, he rips himself free of the other *mikos*' hold and bolts directly for Tarquin. The tattooed boy has little time to react, gaping open-mouthed as the possessed youth closes the remaining distance between them and leaps—

—only to hit an invisible barrier that sits between two of the dolls protecting the circle, knocking him backward. The *mikos* are on him immediately, still chanting, though the boy now seems to possess the strength of ten men. He manages to tear himself away from both Amaya and Saya, and is well on his way to pulling free from Kagura when his whole body suddenly jerks upward, stiffening before falling back lifelessly onto the floor. The *obaasan* has reclaimed the stone knife and, without hesitation, plunges it into the doll's body. A sound much like a heavy slap reverberates around the room. From outside, Callie thinks she can hear a long wail of pain, louder than any the boy has made, before it stops abruptly in mid-scream.

A queer calm descends on Chinsei shrine. Even the birds do not sing.

"It is done," the *obaasan* says wearily. Kagura gently mops at the now-sleeping boy's face with the sage and sweetgrass leaves. "The spirit has left him. When he wakes, he will be just as he was before."

The parents and relatives are effusive with their praise, offering the *obaasan* a few sacks of rice and vegetables, though the fear and awe do not quite leave their faces. It is meager payment for so violent an exorcism, but the *mikos* accept the offerings gratefully, with heartfelt thanks.

"And that is how a person is exorcised." Kagura sighs once the visitors have left. Tarquin is staring with horror at the doll still draped on the floor, with the stone knife still stabbing through where its heart would have been. Its sightless eyes, once devoid of color, are now a deep, burning black. The other mikos are already busy, cleaning the floor with the rest of the sage and the sweet leaves.

"It is a part of the ritual," Kagura tells him, as the *obaasan* picks the doll up and slowly twists the knife out from its chest. She waves it over the stalks of incense several times, murmuring all the while, before placing it inside a different glass case altogether, where other dolls with those same black eyes are kept. "The spirit is now trapped within the doll and shall be fully cleansed at *Obon*."

"I gotta go through that, too, don't I?" Tarquin asks suddenly.

Perhaps in his mind's eye he sees another ritual, one where he is strapped down on the floor, screaming and hurling vile imprecations. But his face is calm, as if he has already accepted this fate. "That's how *Obaasan* is going to exorcise the ghost out from me."

"If it comes down to it, will you agree?" The *obaasan*'s eyes are boring into his, a strange hush in her voice. Callie feels angry. It is too much to ask a young boy to accept such a horrible task so freely, and she opens her mouth to protest.

"It's okay, Callie," Tarquin says with a serenity that surprises her. "If this is what it takes to get her out, then I guess that's what I have to do."

"Brave boy," the *obaasan* says softly, stroking his head with a smile. "Always, always you have been so brave. I promise that the ritual will be quick, and that you will not remember any of it, if this is of any consolation. Tomorrow is an auspicious date, the best day to perform the ritual. Do not worry, Tarquin-kun. It will be over soon enough."

"I seriously doubt it," Tarquin mutters to himself.

Dinner that night is a feast of flavor. To celebrate the successful exorcism, Kagura has cooked several more dishes than the shrine's usual, simple fare—fragrant *onigiri*, balls of rice soaked in green tea, with *umeboshi*—salty and pickled plums—as filling. There is eggplant simmered in clear soup, green beans in sesame sauce, and burdock in sweet-and-sour dressing. The mood is festive.

"It is important to approach the next day with a good heart and better spirits," Saya explains and laughs at the pun. Tarquin eats more than his fair share and shows little concern for what the next day may bring for him, instead laughing along with the others as the *mikos* tell jokes and recount funny experiences, for even living in the wilderness, there are still many stories to tell. When the meal is over, the *mikos* gather up the dishes, and Tarquin remains by the small porch, staring out into the world outside the shrine. His face is neither worried nor uneasy nor frightened, but curiously thoughtful.

"I could die tomorrow, couldn't I?" he asks Callie, who sits with him. "Something could go wrong with the ritual, and I could die."

"Don't be silly, Tarquin," Callie says, though her thoughts run along those same lines. "The *obaasan* knows what she's doing."

"It could happen. If it was going to be easy to get rid of her, they would have held that ritual for me days ago. Definitely before performing the ritual for that other boy."

"Maybe they just needed more preparation."

"I'm not afraid," Tarquin says. "Isn't that weird? But I'm not afraid anymore. I think it would be a relief to get rid of her, whatever happens. If anything goes wrong tomorrow, can you promise me something, Callie?"

"Nothing is going to go wrong, Tarquin."

"Well, if it does, tell Dad I'm really sorry and that it's not your fault I died. And it might not be so bad, anyway, dying."

"You are *not* going to die. I will protect you every way I can. I promise you that much."

Tarquin smiles up at her, though it is clear he does not believe Callie. "Whatever you say, cuz."

"Do you think Okiku can beat her?" he asks again, much later. The light evening sky has deepened into twilight, and the only source of light in this darkness are the few candles the *mikos* have left for them, bobbing up and down and sending shadows across one wall.

"Beat the woman in black?"

"Kagura-san says the longer someone exists as a spirit, the more powerful they can be. Okiku's ghost has been here for hundreds of years, but the other ghost hasn't. Doesn't that technically make her the one to root for?"

"I think Okiku would have defeated her long before we came here if that was the case. Kagura told me about it. You know that sometimes some gods have more power over some things? Like river gods can only control water, and earth gods can only control earth?"

"If you believe in gods, sure. I guess there's a certain kind of logic to that."

"Well, she thinks that maybe Okiku only has power over abused children, or children in danger, or people who died in the same way she did. Or power over people who murder kids. But not over anything else."

"I guess that kind of makes sense, too. About as much sense as you can get hypothesizing about comparative natural laws that ghosts might follow."

"Like lightbulbs," Callie says with sudden understanding. "And newspaper stacks."

"Lightbulbs?"

"It's nothing important. Something just occurred to me." Callie glances out at the sky. "Maybe it's time to turn in for the night. It's getting pretty late."

"Callie? I was lying. I'm a little scared. But tell anyone else, and I'm gonna deny it and laugh all masculine-like."

"So am I." Callie squeezes his cold hand. Something tells her to look up.

I stand on the ceiling, watching them. Tarquin, too, sees me, but neither show any fear. Oddly enough, he smiles at me and the smile lights up his whole face. "Right, Okiku?"

Tentatively, I smile back.

Callie is less welcoming. Her eyes follow my movements as I drift across the room, disappearing out the window and into the night.

CHAPTER TWENTY

PURIFICATION

Strange dreams keep her company for most of the night.

Callie first imagines she is back in Applegate, teaching a class of students. She can see Tarquin hunched over his desk, drawing, and Sandra, who keeps turning her head to smile at something at the back of the class. There are nine lightbulbs hanging over her head, and as she continues her lecture, they silently explode one after the other. She knows without knowing why that when the last bulb goes out, something will come to take her away.

And then the lightbulbs are inexplicably transformed into long, hanging stalks of hair. She looks up and realizes they are attached to nine women in white, hanging upside down from the ceiling and staring at her with

pale faces

and

bright black eyes.

The dream shifts. Now she finds herself strapped to the gurney inside the Smiling Man's basement, as the murderer methodically cuts off her fingers one by one. And yet she feels no pain and watches placidly as the Smiling Man is enveloped in a mass of hair that tears him into pieces.

Then she is standing before a ring of mirrors. In some, she can see herself looking out. In others, it is Tarquin, his face solemn and grim, or the woman in black, bits of mask still clinging stubbornly to her horrifically disfigured face. In some, I look out at her as a vengeful creature, and in others as a young girl in a servant's garb.

And then she sees Tarquin struggling to free himself, while Yoko Taneda and the masked woman loom over him, the first tracing tattoos on his skin and the other carving them out with a stone knife. He is screaming.

The dream shifts briefly, and she watches me run across a dark, nameless river, running after paper lanterns bobbing in the stream. And then the scene changes again, and now eight dolls are arranged neatly in a circle, and I stand inside it. As she looks on, I move around the ring, laying my hand on each doll.

"One."

"Two."

With each count, I change. My hair comes undone, more of it falling over my eyes.

"Three."

"Four."

The obi slips away, my kimono coming loose and undone as blood seeps into the fabric.

"Five."

"Six."

My skin loses its color and sags into unhealthy, blotched white.

"Seven."

"Eight."

And I disappear. Only the circle of dolls remains.

It is only then Callie realizes I am behind her, my hands burrowing into her yellow locks, warring with the thin black strands of my own.

"Nine,"

I whisper into her ear.

Callie looks down at herself. She reaches up at her own head and feels the tangle of disheveled hair, the glassy sheen of her own complexion and realizes that the horrifying visage in the mirror is not mine, but her own face.

"Yes,"

she says.

And then Callie starts awake, white-faced and trembling. It is lighter outside, two hours away from dawn, but she crawls out onto the porch, waiting for the sun until it breaks through the horizon, comforting her. When she looks to her left, I am sitting beside her, dressed as the servant I had been in my youth, with my eyes glued to the sky.

"Will Tarquin die?" Callie asks aloud, though she does not address this question to me. "Is he going to die today?"

This, I cannot answer.

The sunrise over Yagen Valley is beautiful. The air is crisp, and birds fly overhead, dotted against sky the color of peaches and lavender.

There is much to do for the ritual. All participants must first be purified, and Tarquin is embarrassed, turning away quickly, while the *mikos* show no qualms at taking off their clothes and bathing at what they call the *Chinsei-no-yu* hot springs, and they laugh at his flushed face. Taking pity on him, Callie brings him to the second *onsen* spring, where he is able to bathe and rest with none of the other teasing *mikos* for company. For Callie, the water feels unusually hot against her skin, a pleasant warmth that penetrates into her very being. *If only everything could be this way—like a river*, she thinks, *where all things warm and light can float on forever*.

After the hot springs, Tarquin is given a faded but comfortable *yukata* to wear. Callie herself wears a loose, formfitting cotton kimono Kagura lends her. Every stitch of clothing that the participants wear must also be purified and cleansed beforehand, down even to the socks on their feet. Already the other *mikos* are hard at work. They scrub down the altars, the wooden floors and walls, even the movable shoji screens, with sprigs of sage and more sweetgrass, even going so far as to wash the wooden porch and parts of the roof with sage and sweetgrass before sprinkling everything with more salt.

Kagura explains that the combination of sage and sea salt dispels the negativity of a particular place, while sweetgrass encourages positivity to settle in once the negativity has dispersed. The *mikos* perform this cleansing three times, once every hour, to ensure its maximum potency.

The ritual makes use of not one, but eight dolls, carefully selected from the display. "These are the best of the dolls we have," the *obaasan* says. The old woman appears to be in a good mood, even as her gnarled but still nimble fingers rip the dolls open, emptying their cotton contents into a small wooden bowl. Another larger bowl bearing fragrant rice grains, blessed earlier that day, sits on her right side, and as in the previous exorcism, they will serve as filling.

"These dolls have been with us the longest, and so they have borne witness to numerous rituals and purifications, have soaked up the holiness of Chinsei. Some have been with the shrine for more than a hundred years. We use these dolls in groups of eight when we purify especially powerful demons, you see."

"Will they be able to hold someone as powerful as Chiyo?" Callie asks her.

"They should. We had very few reasons to attempt this before Chiyo died." With that chilling revelation, the old woman stuffs the rice grains, then takes up needle and red thread to expertly stitch the dolls close. "But today is a very auspicious day. I have much hope." She winds the excess threads around each doll's body, keeping them firmly in place.

"My sisters and I will all take part in the ritual," Kagura explains further. "Technically, a *miko* who is strong enough can carry out the ritual herself, but more will strengthen it. It is better to be safe than to be sorry."

The *mikos* also do other things they did not do for the seven-year-old's exorcism. Kagura and Amaya have been up earlier than the others to make several more necessary purchases in Mutsu. Now Callie watches as Saya smears a liberal amount of sea salt onto the only two mirrors inside the shrine, to the extent that her own reflection is now barely visible. The shrine maiden stops by the doorway leading into the next room.

"Okiku-sama," she says aloud. "You must step out of the room for now and allow us to complete the ritual successfully."

She then tosses several handfuls of the salt along the entrance. More is added in a straight and unbroken line around the corners of the room to prevent any malingering spirits from escaping or entering once the ritual begins.

Every conceivable bowl or container found inside the shrine is filled with water, and even more sea salt is added to them: eight serving bowls, two plugged sinks, five wooden buckets, four of the incense burners that would not be used that day. Even the small wooden spoons the *miko* use for their daily meals (six) are spread across a tatami mat, the hollow curves filled with as much water as they can hold. Finally, Amaya hands Callie four pieces of sage and requests that she put half of these in her mouth, and the other half on the soles of her feet, which she does by slipping them inside her socks.

Finally, all eight dolls are ready. They are brought out to form a large circle in the center of the room, with equal amounts of more sweetgrass in between each doll. The *obaasan* gestures at Tarquin, who has said nothing all morning, silently watching the preparations.

"*Obaasan* wants you to take off your *hakama*," Kagura translates. "Lie down at the center of these dolls, and remain perfectly still."

Whatever nervousness and unease Tarquin experienced the night before is now gone. His face is quietly composed, and he shows little fear. Dutifully, he stands in the middle of the dolls' ring. Dutifully he removes his hakama, revealing the vile seals he has sought to keep hidden for all of his short life. Of the five, three of the seals have faded to be nearly invisible against his skin, while one remains a deep black. Still another seems uncertain, fading from black to transparent and back again.

Dutifully, Tarquin lies on his back, his palms turned toward the ceiling. His breathing is heavy. Around him, the other *mikos* settle themselves outside of the circle, kneeling and positioned so that each *miko* is within reach of three of the dolls.

The *obaasan* takes the best and the most beautiful of these dolls: an *ichimatsu* in a pure white kimono, with lovely, colorless eyes and soft, silky black hair, and lifts it over Tarquin's head. Slowly, the old woman begins to chant, and the ritual begins.

An hour passes, and then another. Still the *obaasan* continues without stopping, and still the other *mikos* surrounding the circle wait with their heads bowed and their hands folded, never moving.

And yet nothing happens.

But by the third hour it becomes obvious that something has taken hold of the shrine. The small wind chimes that hang by the entrance, greeting each gust and whisper of air that enters, have now fallen silent, barely stirring in the sudden stillness. Something creaks along the floor, though no one moves. Callie, sitting just outside the circle, sees the looser floorboards bend under some unseen weight, as if an invisible foot treads on them. The creaking sounds circle the dolls and the *mikos* beside them, like an invisible beast stalking prey.

If the others are aware of this unseen intruder, they give no sign. But at the *obaasan*'s signal, the other *mikos* begin chanting in unison, a chorus of voices and sutras that crackle through the air with hidden power. The creaking increased in retaliation, an invisible tantrum stamping angrily about.

Callie suddenly understands. The *mikos* and dolls are creating a barrier between Tarquin and the unseen spirit, preventing it from gaining access to his body. Slowly and painstakingly, they are severing her connections to him.

Something begins to scream, but it comes from no physical source. Shriek after shriek rings out, howls of rage echoing up to the nearby mountains. Callie presses herself against one corner, arms clapped around her head to drown out the horrible sounds. And still the *mikos* remain unaffected and chant on. Tarquin stares up at the ceiling, never blinking, and gives no indication he hears the tumult around him.

In time the screams grow weaker, as if the screamer has been drained of most of its strength. At another gesture from the *obaasan,* the chants increase in volume and speed, and the old woman lifts the *ichimatsu* doll over her head, shouting triumphantly. The floor begins to rattle, as does everything inside the Chinsei shrine. Dolls that do not take part in the ritual topple to the floor, cracks appearing in the display glass. Heavy bowls containing water slosh noisily, and from above, a wooden beam actually splits in two, showering sawdust and splinters onto the *mikos* below. Callie gasps, but the shrine maidens have nerves of steel and do not flinch.

Despite the growing violence around them, there is peace within this ring of dolls, and Tarquin remains untouched. The *obaasan* does not waver. The doll remains aloft, and Callie sees how the pupils of its eyes dilate and contract. A cold wind picks up, and the young woman spots a faint figure clad in black struggling against this air, helpless as it is drawn closer and closer to the doll. Inch by grudging inch it gives way, until finally the figure is sucked right into the doll's prim rosebud mouth. Something wails loudly one last time and then stops. The wind dies down, and from outside, the wind chimes ring again.

The *obaasan* has stopped chanting, and so have the other *mikos.* With hands that now betray themselves by their trembling, the old woman sets the doll down beside Tarquin's head. Brief sighs erupt from around the other mikos, sounds of relief. Tarquin does not get up from the floor, however, and stares at something above him. The strange tattoos around his body have finally disappeared.

"It is done," the *obaasan* says with finality. Callie stares at the boy's prone body, unsure why Tarquin does not move, why he does not look like he is breathing.

"Tarquin-kun," Kagura says, "the ritual is over now. You can get up now. See? The tattoos are gone."

And still Tarquin says nothing. The satisfied look on the *mikos'* faces changes abruptly to one of concern when he does not move. His chest does not rise and fall, and he does not blink.

"Tarquin-kun?"

Saya crouches over the prone boy, frowning. And then she gives a small cry of alarm and turns one of his wrists over.

There is one remaining seal on the boy's body, throbbing frantically against his flesh like a heartbeat. It is the seal on Tarquin's left wrist, the same seal bearing Callie's blood. Callie, the only victim to survive the woman's curse.

"What has happened?" The *obaasan* is shocked, trying to rise to her feet.

"The seal is still here!" Saya sounds panicked.

"That is impossible! It should have disappeared along with the others unless…unless…"

The *obaasan's* hard gaze now swivels toward Callie's stunned face.

"It was you, wasn't it?" Callie does not need to understand the woman's Japanese to glean its meaning from the fury of her lips, the anger in her eyes. "It was your blood on this seal!"

"I…I don't…"

"You should have told us, Callie-chan!" Kagura wails. "You

should have told us it was your blood, your seal! Everything that bears witness to the ritual must be pure and untainted. You should have been forbidden to watch!"

"I'm sorry! I…I didn't know…"

There is a loud gasp, and the *obaasan* suddenly stumbles, her face deathly pale. She is clutching at her stomach, where the hilt of a stone knife protrudes. She tries to speak, but blood flows instead from her mouth, and she falls onto the wooden floor.

"Machika-*obaasan*!" Forgetting their duties, the other *mikos* rush to the old woman's side, unmindful of the pool of blood that is spreading from her in spirals, growing larger and larger until it first brushes and then soon immerses itself in Tarquin's hair. The boy's mouth falls open, and a harsh, choking sound comes from his throat.

It is Amaya who is first made aware of the danger. "No!" she howls, attempting to lift Tarquin and bring him away, but by then it is too late. Blood drips onto the boy's back, onto the final untouched seal that reappears on his skin without warning, before just as suddenly dissolving back into nothingness.

The darkness steals into the room, blocking out the daylight outside, and with it comes cold, mocking laughter.

The ritual has failed. The woman in black

is

    free.

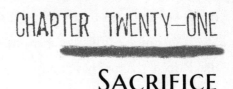

CHAPTER TWENTY-ONE

SACRIFICE

First come the

screams.

In the darkness they come from everywhere and nowhere, all at once.

And then come the terrible sounds of

bodies,

the crunch of bone against wood and stone.

And then there comes the

silence.

When the shadows lift, *she* stands within the ring of dolls, beside Tarquin's prostrate form. The dolls that once surrounded the circle have been thrown with such force that one embeds itself in a wooden wall and another is flung outside and into a tree.

The *mikos* resemble broken dolls themselves. Saya has been tossed several yards into the next room, and only her feet peek out from underneath a shattered wooden screen. Amaya has been driven into the doll glass display. She lies unmoving on the floor, red bleeding out from her head, and many of the dolls have tumbled out, burying her silent form.

Kagura lies in a crumpled heap off to one side, her arms and hands cut and torn from flying glass that has sliced into her skin. She is groaning softly, the only one of the *mikos* to offer proof of life. Parts of the roof have caved in, wood and heavy debris burying the back rooms.

Even Callie, huddled in her corner, the farthest away from the woman's fury, is not without casualty. A heavy wooden plank has fallen from the ceiling, crushing her ankle.

But it is the old woman, the *obaasan*, who suffers worst. She is stretched out on the floor on her stomach, her eyes staring into the wood as the blood seeps from her wounds, pooling around her. In her hand she clutches the *ichimatsu* doll that should have been the woman in black's new prison, though the doll itself is burned nearly beyond recognition, its head lying some distance away.

The woman in black is laughing. Callie scrambles forward despite her injured leg in a desperate bid to protect the unresponsive Tarquin, but an unseen force repels her, pushing her backward. It feels like an electric jolt sizzling into her skin, and she cries out in pain, clutching at her arm as a small burn mark appears across it, shaped like a human hand.

The mask is gone. The woman in black stands before them, and the body that once belonged to the *miko* named Chiyo is a disfigured tragedy. Her bright, sunken eyes look out from the hollows of her face, and her lipless mouth is pulled back to reveal horrible brown teeth, sharp as a canine's. Her hair is a mottled black, a symphony of disorder and disease. Clumps of it fall away from one side of her head to reveal gleaming, ivory bone.

"Tark!" Callie cries out.

The boy does not respond. He is twitching ever so slightly, but his mouth is slack and his eyes lackluster, caught up in the ancient malady, in the web of power the woman in black spins around him. But the creature does not bother to look down at the boy, at the sacrifice she has inhabited for most of his life. Instead, her eyes are on Callie. With painstaking slowness, she lifts a putrefied foot and steps out of the broken circle, to where the girl cowers.

Callie realizes why. The lone seal on Tarquin's body still beats in a silent, horrible cacophony on his left wrist. To be completely free, the woman in black must finish what she started in the Smiling Man's basement.

Holding her injured arm, Callie scrambles away, crying out when pain lances up her foot. She attempts to stand and fails, as the woman in black closes the distance with slow, measured steps, leaving scorched marks along the floor with every step. She stands between the girl and the sliding doors leading outside the shrine, and so Callie has little choice but to crawl over the salted doorway into the next room, desperate to find another way out.

But the woman in black is so very near that Callie can see the frozen expression of hate on what is left of the dead *miko*'s face. She can hear the chopped, ragged

moans

rattling in the corpse's throat, so soft they can almost be mistaken for breathing. She can smell death in that towering form.

The next room has no exit. Crying, Callie presses her back against the wall as the masked woman approaches, cringing as the woman's long decayed hands reach out for her face, nails long and sharpened.

It is then that I

drop

from the ceiling, between Callie and this dead *miko*.

The woman in black draws away, the hissing more apparent, while I stand and do nothing but look back at her with pupil-less eyes. The shadows around the woman rise, lashing at the air like an angry viper.

I do not back down. I do not move away.

She changes prey and lunges at me. I slide away, and she passes harmlessly through. She spins around as I reappear behind her and grab at the dead woman's hair, tearing through the stringy mass with ferocious satisfaction. Her snarls grow louder, and she swipes at me with a clawed hand.

I have never been attacked by spirits of my own kind before, and so I do not know what to expect. The cut the black-robed *miko* administers is not physical in nature, yet it sends a sharp, biting agony through me all the same. I have lived hundreds of years longer, but the dead *miko* has housed numerous demons and spirits within her during her short lifetime, and their combined strength stems from thousands of years of enmity. They are like poison running through her body, fueling it and giving her decayed form existence.

And power.

I give ground, and the dead *miko* senses her advantage. She lunges again, the momentum sending us both hurtling into the wall, but I alter direction in mid-fall, so that we pass through the mirror instead.

The human eye is not built to follow the movements of the dead, and all Callie views is a series of blurs between the woman in white and the woman in black. But while I pass easily through the salted mirror, the dead *miko* does not. The glass slams into her, and the earth reels from the force, strong enough to send more of the roof tumbling down. The reflected surface with its sea salt prevents her from leaving, a restriction determined by the ritual long before she appeared, and it does not apply to me.

But Callie has not been stagnant throughout this fight. She is crawling back into the main room. She ignores the injured and the dead, and hunts instead for the ritual dolls lying strewn about.

"One." She gasps out, finding one doll and setting it down nearby, within easy reach. "Two." She picks up another, sets it down beside the first.

The salt from the mirror has burned into the dead *miko*'s eyes. She is snarling, and her rage makes her even more dangerous. When I emerge from the floorboards, she is on me in an instant, tearing into me again, and the

pain

from her

hands

is overwhelming. I fight back, grabbing at her feet, and she falls. Immediately, I am on her, my fingernails burrowing into the hollows of her eyes. She is screaming and no longer in triumph.

"Seven!" By now there are dolls lined neatly along the floor, a disturbing contrast to the carnage and blood nearby. And still Callie painfully crawls on to the eighth, which has been thrown outside the shrine, caught in the low branches of a nearby tree. Grabbing onto some tall shrubs, she lifts herself up, hobbling on one foot and attempting to reach up for the doll.

Another scream echoes through the air, and it makes me pause. Tarquin is awake and in pain. He is pawing at his eyes, hands contorted in agony. I remember that his ties to the dead *miko* remain, and that the sufferings I inflict on her body that she can endure may also be those that he cannot.

The dead *miko* takes the opportunity to strike back, as I hesitate in my indecision. With surprising strength, she sends me hurtling into the opposite wall, the wood actually tearing from the brutality.

"Please please please." It is Callie. She is tiptoeing as far as her injuries allow her to, but her fingertips only brush against the sole of the doll's foot, still out of reach. "Oh please oh please oh please oh please…"

Sharp hurt burns in the calves of her legs. The dead *miko* has latched onto Callie's foot. I can hear the girl screaming. The woman relishes the cries. The doll falls to the ground, jarred free by the violent motions, but the girl has been dragged away, pressed against the shrine well with the dead *miko* looming over her. Black bile pours from the gouges I have made in her eyes, now burning in triumph. She pulls her hand back, nails razor-sharp, prepared to deliver the final, killing blow.

"No!"

It is Tarquin. He is awake and has taken hold of the stone knife, its bloody tip set against his neck.

"You thought of killing me once, before Okiku stopped you," he pants. "But you couldn't risk it, could you? That's what they do at the *Obon* festival—they *burn* the possessed dolls. To 'kill' them. That's why Mom's been trying to kill me for the last several years. If I die now, I can at least take you to hell with me."

"Tark," Callie chokes. "No!"

The dead *miko* twitches in his direction.

"Shut up, Callie. Let me handle this." The boy's grip firms, and the knife begins to slice through his skin.

No!

Something knocks his hand away, the knife skittering to the floor.

From inside the well, arms come up to wrap protectively around Callie at the last instant, shielding her when the dead *miko* strikes. When the ghost makes another attempt, I catch her hand easily with my own, and crush it. The hand disintegrates, crumbling into ashes, and she falls back. I move, placing myself between Callie and the spirit, as pure water falls around my form. The dead *miko* is a creature of fire, and it is with fire that she is at her deadliest. But I am a creature of water, of the movement and

flow of

tides and rivers, the

depths of stagnant pools. I,

too, can be deadly.

Callie crawls away, now bruised and bleeding heavily, but I continue my attack, slashing at every part of the dead woman that I can reach. The well must have been purified by the other *mikos*, or was consecrated to *kami* at some time in the past, for the waters burn their way through the dead *miko's* body flesh whenever my nails score; sizzling like acid, stripping away her physical flesh. It is then that I see the demons festering inside the dead *miko's* body, the repugnance of creatures that have feasted on her mind and body for so long that not even a glimmer of who she was and what she could have been can be seen. I look in and I see

hate, creeping hate little sputters mad mad feed must feed will feed always feeding

hungry screamscreaming ripping twisted twisting never fear all fear hating hating

all always hating little corners little corners rip through quivering skin laugh

clawing fester sour little skin corpse quiet skin hate we hate hate die die die die

true madness.

I see now that even the dead *miko's* face is a mask, her body a farce for the demons hiding within to play at human. It is a fate worse than even the one I have endured, but I have little time to feel pity. These demons of filth howl from beyond the *miko*'s undead husk and look out at me through the empty shells of her eyes.

Not even the severity of her wounds can distract Callie. Clutching at her side, where the cloth of her kimono is now stained a crimson red, she half staggers, half limps to the eighth doll, finding it and adding it to the line of dolls she has started. Now, she counts again.

"One sacrifice! Two, three, four, five!" She places her hand on every doll as she goes down the line. The dead *miko* is unaware of her intent, but I comprehend her purpose. The woman continues to struggle, unable to break free from my grip, but the water from the well has given me strength, and she is powerless to escape.

"Eight sacrifices!" And then Callie turns to us, locked in our dreadful battle. Perhaps we will spend the balance of our existence in this manner—one unable to break free, and the other holding on at the cost of everything else.

She points at the dead *miko*, and fear bursts through her voice. "Nine! Nine sacrifices!"

It is a truth that the other *mikos*, even the old woman, for all her wisdom, have overlooked.

Words in themselves have their own power. When Callie named the ninth sacrifice, the power in those words transferred itself to me.

And I

    respond.

The small demons that feed around the dead *miko*, the shadows that call attention to her presence, are the *shivering whimper feed feeding hate hatred hating*

    creeping seek seeking flesh flee snapping hate

first to fall. I tear through them like shredded paper, my teeth ripping through. Then it is the larger demons' turn, the ones that lurk behind her eyes, and I plunge my hands through those twin

whisper whispering screaming screaming mine mine

    arms legs tear limbs fear hate hate mine flee mine

sockets, rending everything I find. Finally, I attack the mask herself. I rip through the husk, into centuries of forgotten filth and malice. I plunge my hands into the dead *miko's* stomach, rending and rupturing

hate hate hate hate die why die die why die die die

    die die die die die why die die die die die die die

all that I can until, against all odds, I see a faint shimmer of light, a whisper of innocence, a small, forgotten firefly trapped for years within that seething mass.

Somewhere within that malignant spirit, little bits of Chiyo Takeda still cling, waiting for the day she is free to finish the task she set out to do. Perhaps it is because of her close resemblance to her younger sister, Yoko, that I see a little of Tarquin on her sad, youthful face. She looks at me, and I know what she is asking.

And so does Callie. She stumbles forward, the stone knife in her hands, but she only takes a few more steps before her strength finally gives out. She drops down, the blade skittering to rest by my feet.

I

     pick

it up.

There is regret in Chiyo Takeda's face, grief at her failure, yet hopefulness for a last chance at redemption. I carry out her last request and plunge the stone knife into the dead miko's heart.

"Ten," I hear Callie whisper.

And all around me the air

explodes

into

little

     fireflies.

CHAPTER TWENTY—TWO

APPEASEMENT

"Am I dead?" she asks me. I do not answer.

There is a funeral in the distance. There are twenty-seven men, twenty-six women, and three children. There are four pallbearers and one priest. The sun is shining, but the grass smells like rain. They are lowering a simple silver coffin into the ground, and everyone watches. No one is smiling, and a few people cry.

"Is that me?" she asks again. "Am I dead?" Still I do not respond.

Unexpectedly, there is laughter from across the field. She turns her head and sees children. They are dressed in white, and they are running, laughing. There could be sixty of them or two hundred or a thousand. They are too innumerable to count. They are humming something, a soft, familiar lullaby.

She tries to join them, but she cannot. She is wearing too much red. A scarlet stain blossoms along her waist, spreading like watercolors across a linen canvas. She is wearing far too much red.

There is a hot spring at the end of the field. Without knowing why, she finds herself stumbling toward it, knowing instinctively that this is where she must go. There are no changing rooms here, and to step into the *onsen*, she must undress.

There is nothing to be ashamed of. She removes her clothes. There is a terrible wound on her hip, a slight pain when her hands wander into the area. But the pain feels muted somehow, like hurt is of no consequence here. Slowly she steps into the water. It feels hot and cold and good against her skin, and the small throbbing leaches out of her, the waters tinged now with pink.

She looks up and sees me, fully clothed, in the water before her. Neither I nor my clothes are wet, and she knows there is something wrong with this, though it is getting very hard to think.

"Am I dead?" she asks again.

I do not speak, but I dip my hands into the water, cupping and pouring the clear liquid over her head. As if on her own accord, Callie sinks under the bubbling surface, immersing herself in the comforting warmth.

When she resurfaces, the meadow and the children are gone, though the lullaby continues. She is floating in a river surrounded by darkness as far as the eye can see. There is nobody else around, and fear grips her.

"Hello?" she calls out, and the sound only echoes, her voice bouncing off unseen barriers.

It is then that she sees the fireflies.

They appear in twos and threes, winking back at her over the dark waters, and then in half dozens and dozens, and then in droves, until all around her a million fireflies blink in and out over the night sky, like paper lanterns that bob up and down in the air.

From within their glow she could see tiny snatches of life. Children's laughter rings out, small happy faces drifting in and out of the fireflies' light. There are faces of redheads and blondes and brunettes, of Japanese and American and French, African and Indian and Greek. There are eight-year-olds and four-year-olds and eleven-year-olds and fifteen-year-olds. There are shy smiles and gap-toothed grins.

They gather around her, tiny balls of fire fluttering close to her head, soft wings light and feathery, brushing against her cheek.

From somewhere above them, another light beckons. It looks like nothing more than a distant star at first, a white sphere of dust in the heavens. But soon it grows in size and brightness, until the whole breadth of sky opens up into that white light, turning night into day in an instant.

At some unspoken signal, the fireflies flit around Callie one last time and then soar joyfully upward, spiraling above her in slow, lazy circles. They do not stop until they touch the bright white light, disappearing into radiance.

More fireflies beat their wings against her forehead, and Callie thinks she can make out the smiling shapes of Amaya, and even the old *miko*, within their glows. Amaya looks nearly a teenager, and even the *obaasan*'s white hair is now a glossy black. The wrinkles on her face disappear, leaving her young and at peace. They circle Callie one last time before lifting their wings to join their brother and sister lights.

Two figures walk across the water toward her, shining as brightly as hundreds of the fireflies at once. One is a face Callie has seen before. Yoko Taneda is happier here, her face unlined by the harshness of time, shoulders unburdened by the memories of grief. Beside her stands a taller, older woman, who bears striking physical similarities to her sister. But where her tainted spirit had once garbed itself in robes of black, fettered by the company of demons, Chiyo Taneda stands dressed in a soft white, and on her face is the same sense of joy that fills her sibling's expression. They are holding hands and smiling down at Callie, floating in the water, and she feels the softest of touches, like invisible fingers brushing across her mind.

"Thank you," they whisper and turn away. They glow brighter, and when the light finally diminishes, they join the other children as another pair of tiny fireflies, their illuminations perhaps a shade brighter than those around them, as they begin their journey up into that sacred light.

Callie watches in awe as these flights of souls continue their upward loop into the shining sky, until most of the fireflies have passed through into that inviting warmth. She senses another presence behind her and turns to see me standing on a nearby shore, watching the fireflies' ascent. I am dressed in the kimono I had once worn in younger, older days, back when *chochin* once floated along the rivers of my hometown, back when I, in my youthful ignorance, once chased after them, hoping in my foolishness that I could follow them into forever.

"Okiku?" she finds herself asking. I remain silent, and perhaps something in my eyes—the sorrow perhaps, or the wistful regret—makes her repeat herself with more urgency. "Okiku? What about you? Why aren't you leaving with them?"

I do not move. I do not make my own step into the water, do not dream about turning into

fire

that

flies.

Callie swims toward me, struggling in the still-dark river, believing that she can somehow make me see. "Go into the light, Okiku! Go with them!" The last of the fireflies have gone, and the heavens now begin to weaken and lose their brilliance. She fears that soon they will close up and leave me standing alone by the shore.

"Okiku! Please!"

And when her hands finally touch the edges of soil, and she looks up to plead with me once again, she sees the change in my appearance. Gone are the kimono and the white obi tied around my waist, and gone are the simple ornaments that I weave into my hair, as I did for *chochin* festivals during my once-life. Gone is the wistful expression, the desire to step out and join these little fireflies in the bright unknown. Instead, my dead spirit looks back down on her: my bloodied robes and knotted locks of hair, the mangled neck and sightless eyes. Callie recoils, stricken.

"Where they go,"

I say, and the words issue out from bloodless, unmoving lips,

"I

cannot

follow."

"But can't you try?" Callie cries. "You deserve to go just as much as they do!"

I kneel on the shore so she in the water can better see my ghastly, swollen face, my distended limbs.

"There is something else I must do," I say, before reaching to touch her face with my cold, dead hand.

Callie jerks awake, suddenly aware of someone bending over her, and briefly she panics, attempting to struggle free.

"She's awake!" someone says.

"Callie-san!" another person cries out, and dimly, Callie recalls knowing this voice.

"Callie-san. This is Kagura. Do you remember? Are you all right?"

Blinding light assails her vision when she opens her eyes, and Callie groans. She feels several people lifting her and setting her back down on something that feels softer and warmer than the hard ground she had been curled up on only moments before. She opens her eyes again, blinking rapidly. The light no longer hurts as much, but instead of the wooden walls and altar, she sees only tall trees around her, the sun peeking in through the canopy. She hears the louder sounds of rushing water, and she sees the area now filled with strangers dressed in pristine white. *They are coming to take me away to Remney's, too*, she thinks, and suppresses the hysterical giggles threatening to burst through her lips.

"Callie-san," Kagura says again, and Callie latches on to the familiarity of her voice, the genuine worry in her tone. "These are medical personnel from Mutsu. They're going to put you inside their ambulance and bring you to the hospital, so you can be treated for your injuries. Do you understand me?"

Callie's side feels stiff and numb, but she also feels something prodding at her side, trying to stanch the blood. She can see Kagura bending over her, looking pale and exhausted. The *miko*'s face has been cut badly, and her left eye is black and swollen.

"Tark," Callie mumbles. "Where is Tark?"

Another head appears beside Kagura's. It is the boy himself, looking just as worn and tired, but alert. Save for his bruises and his bandaged neck, he shows no other signs of injury.

"Callie," he gasps out.

But Callie only smiles at him, relieved to see he is all right. "What about the others? *Obaasan* and Saya and Amaya?"

"Saya has a broken arm and leg, and she has a bad concussion, but the doctors think she will be all right. But for the others…" At this Kagura pauses and sadly shakes her head.

"I am sorry," Callie whispers. Tarquin squeezes her hand.

"It is done. Chiyo's spirit has been appeased, and that is what they would have wanted. I can only hope their spirits, too, are finally at rest."

"Like fireflies," Callie whispers.

"This is all my fault," Tarquin says. On his arms and chest, all traces of the binding seals have disappeared.

"You are as much a victim as any of us, Tarquin-kun. Perhaps even more so..."

A male voice interrupts, talking in Japanese and sounding apologetic. The voices fade out, and Callie now feels herself being lifted into a small white van, where more people she does not know gather around her, issuing commands to one another. A small mask is inserted over her nose and mouth, and she takes a deep, grateful breath. She lifts her head, looking out the van's doors, and sees Kagura and Tarquin standing side by side, looking anxiously back at her. Tarquin says something to the *miko*, who nods. He runs toward the van. "Can I ride with her?" he asks. "She's my cousin..."

After a hurried discussion, they allow him inside the ambulance. He holds Callie's hand as she drifts in and out of consciousness, as the van speeds along the small, unused road leading back into the city. Sometimes, when Callie comes to and remembers herself, she glances up at Tarquin, who is smiling encouragingly back, telling her in between the murmurs of the attendants and the squealing of sirens that things will be all right and that his father is going to kill him for all the trouble he'd caused, and she smiles at the reversal in their positions.

Why didn't you go? she wants to ask me, but there is a marked change in the air, and she no longer feels my presence. For the first time since arriving in Japan, she does not feel the burden of spirits around them.

"What's wrong?"

"No, it's nothing…" Callie says and tries to smile again, but soon enough feels herself drifting back to sleep.

The local police conduct a brief search inside Chinsei shrine. My fight with Chiyo had triggered a landslide, and it is the easiest explanation for them to accept. The bodies of the *mikos* yield no further clues, and while Kagura and Saya are held and questioned briefly, they are soon released due to a lack of evidence, their testimonies corroborated. As in my time, many of the people in these parts are of a superstitious nature, particularly in areas around *Osorezan* and Yagen Valley where things occur that sometimes cannot be explained, and the general attitude even among many of the authorities is that the less they meddle in the affairs of the supernatural, the better.

Callie spends the next six days being treated at the hospital and is released just in time to attend the funeral rites of Machika Fukushima and Amaya Kaede, both of whom have been cremated and their ashes strewn to the four winds outside the temple, as they had once done for Yoko Taneda.

"I do not know what will become of the shrine," Kagura tells Callie sadly as they stand by the shrine's small well one morning.

The Chinsei Shrine has been cleaned and most of its roof rebuilt, though a few rooms remain closed off. The display case that houses many of its dolls has been fixed, and it stands again as it once had. Chinsei has survived Chiyo's onslaught, though a sad, strange emptiness lingers.

Already the Bodai Temple at *Osorezan* and the small Yagen Onsen resorts are preparing to close for most of October, opening only when spring arrives and the snow thaws. "Chinsei will need to go through many purification rituals before we can continue. And without *Obaasan* and Amaya-chan, there will only be Saya and me, and we are not skilled enough to carry out the exorcisms that *Obaasan* had accomplished."

"Where will you stay in the meantime?" Callie asks.

"Saya has family in Honshu, and I have an aunt who's invited me to stay with her in Kyoto. We both plan to do as many purification rituals as we are able to until we leave in October, after the *Obon* Festival. We will burn the rest of the possessed dolls, and we will continue the rituals again when spring arrives. For now, we shall spend the rest of this winter healing and mourning"—Kagura smiles sadly—"and then going on. It is what Machika-*obaasan* would have wanted."

Callie looks back at the shrine. Though they will not be allowed inside until after most of the purification rituals are done, it no longer feels threatening to her.

"Tarquin is also something of a miracle," Kagura admits. "I was relieved when he woke up from the ritual unharmed. When a spirit of such malignancy vacates a body, it leaves behind negative energy that can serve as a beacon to other less powerful but still dangerous demons. It would have been necessary to cleanse his body, for his spiritual energy would have been weak.

"But I was surprised by how strong his energy was upon waking." She laughs softly. "In older times he would have been a fine *onmyji* the likes of the legendary Abe no Seimei, especially as he has kept the demons in his body at bay for all these years, far more than any of us ever could have, even Chiyo. With the proper training, he could have made an exceptional Buddhist priest."

"Well, that's nice of her to say," Tarquin says, when Callie tells him. They are standing by the shrine's well, looking down into the darkness, though they see nothing. "I think I'd look pretty good in a robe and those really big hats, too."

They say nothing for a while, waiting by the well and continuing to peer down at its depths, looking for something that still does not appear.

"So," Callie says, "'Shut up, Callie. Let me handle this'? That's your choice for famous last words?"

"I was under a lot of pressure, all right? I'd like to see *you* come up with anything better at such short…" Callie is already laughing, and soon the boy cannot help but join her. But Callie's laughter begins to waver and break, until she now begins to weep, allowing the emotions from the last several months to catch up to her. Tarquin says nothing as she turns and cries on his shoulder. The laughter fades from his expression, and he stares over her shoulder, troubled.

Alarmed and shaken by the recent turn of events, Tarquin's father flies immediately back to Mutsu. He believes the police when they tell him of the landslide, but an inordinate amount of time is spent reprimanding his son for getting Callie into trouble. Surprisingly, the boy endures the lecture meekly enough, and anger eventually gives way to relief and tears. The three soon find their way back to Tokyo. Within a week, they return to America.

For now, the Chinsei shrine remains uninhabited, as almost everything else is in Yagen Valley during the cold months. Nothing moves within its boundaries, and if something does stir within the shrine, within the hundreds of dolls that still lie waiting to be sacrificed, or within those dolls where some things still lurk unseen, struggling futilely to undo the red threads that bind their forms, none go so far as to step out into the daylight and the world beyond. The shrine sits in repose, serene, to await the coming winter and the thawing, healing spring that comes soon after.

CHAPTER TWENTY-THREE

HANAMI

A year passes and, like all humans, they are older.

Callie meets Tarquin and his father for lunch at a small street in downtown Washington, DC, where the Halloways now live. Tarquin is now sixteen. He has grown five inches since Callie last saw him, with every expectation of adding more to his height in the coming months. His skin is darker, and he is quicker now to smile and talk than he was in the past. His natural gift with words has only improved over time, and he regales Callie that week with amusing anecdotes and humorous stories until she is laughing helplessly, pleading with him to stop. He wears a white shirt with short sleeves, and his arms are bare. The tattoos are gone.

Callie is also different. She is studying at a college in Boston and, like the Halloways, no longer lives in Applegate. She wears a long dress that reaches her knees, styles her hair shorter, and still has that scar on her little finger. She is on a scholarship, studying things that sound bigger than their purpose: a degree in education, with a minor in international and cultural studies. She does not always have time to see Tarquin, though they correspond frequently through emails and often arrange for small trips when one can visit the other. Today it is Callie's turn, and after lunch they make their way to the Washington Monument, where the National Cherry Blossom Festival is about to begin.

"I don't know why they don't just call it *hanami*," Tarquin's father says. Of the three, the man is the most unchanged, though he has a faint stoop to his shoulders and a few more lines around his eyes.

Tarquin rolls his eyes. "This isn't Japan, Dad. It's an American thing now, so the general public will probably take 'cherry blossom festival' over a Japanese word they don't understand."

"Maybe I'm just too much of a purist."

"I know. Mom probably said the same thing." There is no longer any anger or fear in his voice when Tarquin refers to his dead mother.

But the National Cherry Blossom Festival viewing takes a backseat to what they call the National Cherry Blossom Festival Parade. Dancers (sixty) litter the streets, holding various symbols and representations of *sakura* blossoms (sixty) over their heads as they prance down the street. Floats of differing sizes and shapes sail past the onlookers, thirty-nine in all, and giant helium balloons (twenty-eight) soar overhead, blocking out snippets of sky as they pass. Marching bands (fifteen) wail out an accompaniment, one of the many sources of entertainment to the crowds that pack the roads, nearly three thousand on this street alone.

Callie and the Halloways spend several minutes watching the

parade before deciding to slip away. Though the parade is pleasing to the eyes, none of them are comfortable in the thick of crowds, and they retreat to lesser populated areas where vendors (twenty) hawk Japanese delicacies to mark the occasion.

There are signs here that say "12th Street" and "Pennsylvania Avenue," and between them lies the *Sakura Matsuri*, the Japanese Street Festival. The three pay the required fee to enter and wander among the small stalls. Most of the people are watching seven martial arts experts practice their respective disciplines. There are three stages in the six blocks allocated for the festival, which will soon host a vast number of performances by musicians and singers. Tarquin's father purchases *takoyaki* balls for them, and for several minutes they stand, watching and chatting and taking in the scenes set before them.

"We should do stuff like this more often," Tarquin muses, several hours later. His father had wandered off to haggle with a nearby vendor for a small replica of a samurai sword. Dusk is beginning to settle, but the crowds are as thick as ever, awaiting the fireworks set to begin in another hour's time.

"College has been tough," Callie admits, "but I should be free for the summer."

Tarquin makes a face. "Isn't summer when you college students go to beaches and drink beer and post your little duckface photos on Facebook?"

Callie knew she should disapprove but laughs instead. "I think someone's going to need to talk with your father about the kind of things you've been watching."

Tarquin is about to make another retort but then falls silent as they pass a small stall that sells different varieties of Japanese dolls, from *ichimatsu* to *musha ningyo* warrior dolls to small Noh figures. Callie follows his gaze and understands, her fingers idly drifting back to her scar, as still is her habit.

"Did you ever hear news from Kagura-chan?" Tarquin asks suddenly.

"She and her aunt moved to Honshu, and they're running a small inn there. She and Saya go to the Chinsei shrine every now and then to put things in order and clean up. I guess there are too many painful memories there for them to stay long. Has she contacted you?"

"Once," Tarquin says. "Dad and I took another trip to Japan a couple of months ago. Even stayed at their bed-and-breakfast for a few weeks."

"Really? What—"

A roar fills the air. Two combatants fight each other with large *kendo* sticks, their faces encased in odd steel masks. The speed and ferocity in the way they attack, and the agility with which they dodge blows by their opponent, draw hearty applause from nearby onlookers.

"The dolls will need a lot of tending," Tarquin says suddenly, after the audience has quieted. "That's what Kagura says. They say they can't have any more spirits breaking out."

Callie has to smile. "I'm sure they know what they're doing. Remember Kagura mentioning you would make a fine *onmyji* if you'd lived in ancient Japan?"

"I looked that up. I'm not so sure I'd do well with the calendar-making and the astrology part of the job, though. Can you imagine me coming up with horoscopes for the emperor? 'Today shall be your lucky day, so long as you don't behead your favorite court *onmyji* for no reason. Girls might like you better if you had a different face, but remember that patience is a heavenly virtue. Also, don't forget about the not-beheading thing.' Maybe I'd like to take a stab at kicking ghosts out of people myself. I've been doing a lot of research into those esoteric Japanese rituals."

"Are you sure that's wise?"

"Dad always says the more you know about something, the better you can plan and protect yourself. So that's what I've been doing."

In the next shop someone is selling *ukiyo-e*. One of these wall scrolls is of a young girl. Her arms are stretched out in front of her, the wrists dangling loosely, and her face is of a preternatural calmness, touched slightly by sorrow. There is a bluish cast to her skin, and she is slowly rising up from a well.

"You like this one? This from *Thirty-Six Ghosts*, one of Tsukiyoka Yoshitoshi's greatest masterpieces," the vendor says proudly in broken English.

"I think I'll take it," Tarquin decides.

He turns to look back into the crowd, and Callie gasps when I raise my head briefly past Tarquin's to look back at her. Nothing about me has changed, except now I seem to rise up from somewhere below Tarquin's chest. With my broken neck, it almost appears as if Tarquin and I are two heads sharing one body.

"Tark!"

"What?" Tarquin glances back at me, puzzled, and I retreat back into his frame. "What's wrong, Callie?"

"You see her, don't you?" Callie is excited, frightened. She had thought that memories of old ghosts would fade over time rather than linger in the present. In the past year she has seen no abnormalities of the senses, no other ghosts that haunt her vision, and she assumed the worst was over.

"Okiku?" Tarquin does not seem surprised. On the contrary, he is calm. Accepting.

"Tark, I know she protected us, but no good can come from keeping her with you. We need to get help—"

"I don't really have much of a choice, Callie," Tarquin says quietly.

"I don't understand…"

"Kagura explained everything to me. Something went wrong in the ritual. With me. I shouldn't have survived, she said. Not given how it ended. She thought I lived because I had enough spiritual energy inside me to make it through, and some other things I didn't really understand. And then she tried to cleanse me again, a pretty simple ritual. Just in case, she said."

And at this Tarquin pauses.

"She's inside me, Callie. She's been here ever since. There had to be something to fill the void that dead woman left in me, and the alternatives Kagura presented were either my dying or my being possessed by some other spirit who wouldn't be as nice about all this as Okiku has been. I don't have the seals anymore, and this is all strictly voluntary on her part—and on mine—so I don't think I can call this a possession. I know *she* doesn't."

Too late, Callie finally understands the terrible decision I made on the banks of that unnamed river, while the fireflies glittered in the darkness, dancing up into the light. Now she understands why I did not follow the other souls into appeasement, despite her urging.

"Okiku and I have had a few talks since then—if you consider conversations with a three-hundred-year-old ghost talking. She doesn't mind hanging around long enough for me to get my karmic groove back or die of natural causes—whichever comes first." Tarquin has the audacity to grin.

"She's a nice spirit, though. She doesn't mind that I don't always clean my room, and she respects my privacy every time I need to go to the bathroom. I've spent a good part of my life living with a horrible, terrible ghost, Callie. Living with Okiku is like a reprieve, in comparison. For the first time in a long, long time, I'm actually happy. I don't go to bed afraid anymore. And I'm pretty sure if there are any other spirits around hoping for a free ride, she'd be more than happy to kick their asses for me."

"I don't think this is something you should be trivializing, Tark."

He squeezes her hand. "I'll be okay, Callie. And thank you for being concerned—for always looking out for me. It's not like I have much choice, but if I had to choose to cohabit with any one spirit in the world, I'd choose her any day."

"Tarquin, Callie, it's getting late," his father calls out. "Do you guys prefer sushi or *okonomiyaki*?"

"How about both?" Tarquin counters. He pays the vendor and accepts the rolled-up scroll. "I think Okiku will appreciate having this on the wall."

"Tark…"

"I don't want to die, Callie. You understand that, right?"

The girl nods. "But there has to be another way."

Tarquin smiles again, but this time it is the smile of one who made peace with his inner demons long ago. "Come on. Dad's waiting."

The teenager walks on ahead, waving to his father. Behind him, Callie can see the figure of a woman in white, flimsy and transparent at first, but eventually gaining substance and shape, keeping pace beside him. She watches as Tarquin turns toward the apparition and offers her his arm. She watches the figure hesitate before, haltingly, accepting it with a pale, withered hand.

This same apparition turns her head slightly, and Callie can make out the startling black eyes, the sunken cheeks, and the jagged cut of mouth that curves into hints of a smile as I bow my head gently in her direction before turning away.

I am the fate that people fear to become. I am what happens to good persons and to bad persons and to everyone in between. I am who I am.

But when you have resigned yourself to an eternity filled with little else but longing, to sacrifice what lies beyond that eternity for one boy's lifetime—it is enough.

Tarquin and I make our way past the shops and past the laughter, leaving Callie standing there alone in the crowd while up above, stars look down from the darkening sky and slowly, as they were born to do, begin to shine.

ACKNOWLEDGMENTS

This book has gone through the hands of many people who believed in its potential and cheered me on every step of the way. I can never be grateful enough.

To my parents—thank you for being my first librarians; for the bookshelves in your bedroom filled with the things I was technically too young to read. To *Papa*, the first writer I know, and to *Mama*, who tried to point me down the right path and who, for the most part, succeeded.

For my sister Kim, who talked me into writing her high school English Lit papers, because she had that much faith—thanks for the practice.

A big thank-you to my cousins—Gin, Dara, Kurt, Timmie, Micah, and Keisha. You were in many ways the Tarquins to my Callie.

Thanks, Eugene, for the words of encouragement that came with every dinner, and also to Stephanie, who believed before I'd ever written a word. All my love to Sars, Nichole, Rip, Sophie, and Sara, for making it fun.

For my amazing agents, Rebecca Podos and Nicole LaBombard, who have championed Okiku's story from day one. Thank you for taking a chance on us, and for loving her as much as I do.

My deepest gratitude to Leah Hultenschmidt for her infectious enthusiasm, and to my editor, Steve Geck, for his wonderful insights and assistance. I will always be grateful to the amazing team at Sourcebooks for everything they've done to make this book a reality. Todd, Cat, Aubrey, Jillian, and everyone else—you all rock.

And finally—to my husband, Les, who didn't give up when I nearly did. This one's for you.

ABOUT THE AUTHOR

Rin Chupeco once wrote obscure manuals for complicated computer programs, talked people out of their money at event shows, and did many other terrible things. She now writes about ghosts and fairy tales, but is still sometimes mistaken for a revenant. *The Girl from the Well* is her first novel.